ALAN AGNEW

Home for Truths

Suicide, Suspicion and Silence

First published by The Imperial Press 2020

This novel is entirely a work of fiction. The names, characters and incidents portrayed in it are the work of the author's imagination. Any resemblance to actual persons, living or dead, events or localities is entirely coincidental.

First edition

ISBN: 978-1-8380402-2-2

Editing by Kirsty Agnew
Advisor: Mackenzie Littledale
Advisor: Patrick Docherty

This book was professionally typeset on Reedsy.
Find out more at reedsy.com

For my wife, Kirsty,
Love As Always x

"Other things may change us,
but we start and end with family."

Anthony Brandt

Chapter One - The Funeral

I wrote two eulogies for my dad. Not two versions. Two separate accounts of his life. The first is how I want to remember him. The life and soul, gregarious by nature, first to the bar to buy the drinks, would talk to anyone. He would make impromptu speeches when not his party as a show of support and affirmation rather than attention-seeking. A confessed man of the world. He was comfortable talking about most subjects. He was warm. He was genuine. He was admired. He died 30 years ago. The second eulogy is how many of the faces gawping up at me as I stand by the pulpit remember him. He was quiet, grumpy, a recluse. His appearance dishevelled. He died three days ago.

The front row is vacant of any family, and we sing hymns my dad would not recognise. There are no tears, no silent minutes for personal reflection. We leave in an orderly fashion walking past the standard-issue coffin without as much as a pause.

The turnout at the church is generous, reflecting more the monotony of village life rather than respect for my dad. There is little else to do on Tuesday mornings with the library shut and village hall closed for renovation.

Strange faces came to me after the service. 'Hi, Phil Jenkins.' The florist was young, her discrete blonde fringe covering her eyebrows stopping just short of her hazel eyes. She has a warming smile, nestled beneath her high cheekbones, silent features giving her a natural beauty with a soft handshake, putting me at ease instantly. 'I wish I had known this man,' she says sincerely, 'so many here have talked so fondly about him, thank you for choosing our family florist to colour his life.'

Others queued before me to pass on their condolences and to reassure me what a good man he was. How could they say this? I wanted validation, but I knew not to ask, I would only learn about the time he once waved in their direction at the post office or donated a tatty old jumper to the village jumble sale. Only one or two remembered my dad from before.

Roger and Mary were welcome faces amongst the tide of black suits, starched white shirts and grey hair in the pub after the service. Roger, now much thinner in face and body, thinning white hair and boasting sprawling sideburns pointing in every direction. His black suit now two sizes too big. His eyes unrecognisable. Their trademark glint had disappeared, obscured by cataracts, his pupils shrinking in size and void of sparkle. Only his handshake remained as I remember, firm and genuine.

Roger and Mary Knight were best friends of my parents back in the day. I cannot remember many weekends when they weren't all sat around the dinner table, putting the world to rights. The wine would be flowing, plenty of gossiping about the neighbours' gardens, moaning about the traffic, conspiracy theories about the new building in the high street, the volume of debate increasing as midnight neared. Sunday morning, I would be first up for my paper round, met by the aroma of the night before, a perfect pairing to the scene. The fulsome waft of cooking fat and garlic from the kitchen with half rinsed stacked dishes dumped in the sink, lingering cigar smoke from the dining room and the living room consumed by the heady aroma of alcohol lingering from abandoned glasses. Their appearance almost art as the red wine stain blends into the splatter of remaining lipstick and the rings of sticky brandy, creating asymmetrical shapes on the coffee table. The stereo would silently hum, the tape long finished but not switched off. It wasn't just weekends, Roger and Mary were present for every occasion, birthdays, Christmas, Easter, cup final on the TV and of course funerals.

Roger bypassed the 'sorry for your loss' protocol and put the spotlight firmly on me.

'Now then Phil, you looking after yourself lad?' he inquires in his Northern dulcet tone.

It was a loaded question. He would have known from my dad of the supposed slippery slope I had been on ever since my marriage break up. I can only manage a shrug.

'Ah, she was not all that anyway,' as if offering me a platform to rant which I did not need. If anything, I wanted to argue back she was all that, she was fantastic, was too good for me, and when she realised it, she left.

I wish she were by my side, talking to these strangers connected only by postcode. Caroline could talk about climate change or currency fluctuations just as comfortably as she could about growing rhubarb in the allotments. She would put me at ease, by finding some safe ground on which I could small talk when required, she was clever that way, how I miss her right now—these forced conversations, with the script already written.

Roger launched into a perfectly honest monologue about my

dad's lost will to live, and how he'd spoken often about wanting his pain to be finally over, from a time even before the cancer.

I hold my clenched fist deep in my pocket, dad had never mentioned this to me. A punch to the gut would have been more merciful than hearing this now. Maybe he did say, and I hadn't wanted to hear? My dad could feel down, a little depressed sometimes.

I'd visited him in the early days, and we occasionally spoke on the phone, mainly to check in on his wellbeing. *'Good'* was the standard response, drawing an impenetrable veil over his life with one little word. I had accepted his excuses at face value: Empty fridge? The local store had closed early. Messy house? He'd been suffering from a cold. Overgrown garden? He'd lent his tools to a neighbour, who'd promised to return them on a day that never came.

Roger's bluntness continued, the privilege of a 50-year friendship. 'He lost his fight years ago, that's the real cost of injustice, losing your spirit, your peace, and your ability to sleep at night. The death certificate may say cancer, but that was not the cause.' He held his hand on my shoulder. 'If there is anything I can do, please let me know. I can't even imagine how tough it must be for you having lost your mother, your father and of course brother.'

Chapter Two – Jimmy

I still remember the piercing scream of my mum all those years ago. I have heard it a million times since. My mind went into overdrive, trying to calculate what was wrong, dismissing any theories as quickly as they formed. I heard my dad's hurried footsteps. I remember the relief that followed, whatever was wrong dad would fix it.

I was wrong. His scream was a deep guttural roar. I froze as the house fell silent for what seemed like an eternity. The heat of adrenaline racing through my 11-year-old body, shooting to the ends of my palms, causing sweat and a tightness in my stomach. I tried to shout. No sound would come. My mouth was dry, the blood physically draining, and my body unrecognisable.

I found myself fighting my body with my mind. I walked downstairs against my will when all I wanted was to curl up on my bed, turn the lights off and to wake up again. The crying of my parents, such a foreign sound. I could not work out if they were muffling their cries, or my senses had shut down to protect me. I walked through the dining room, conscious I had not taken a breath of air.

As I reached the connecting door to the garage, I caught sight of my mum held tightly in my dad's arms; both collapsed on the floor. Our eyes met, they were drained of their natural blue colour, and flooded by tears, then suddenly reforming as they met my gaze, like a fish returning to the water. The tears emptied down her cheeks, and her pupils sparked as she leapt to her feet, tossing my dad to the floor and ran towards me, pouncing like a cheetah on its prey. She slammed the door shut.

The blast of the door physically awoke me from the deepest of dreams, yet I was already awake. My young mind could only process a little at a time, and I felt rejected and abandoned.

Fight or flight.

I ran for the door and out of the house. Our neighbour, Donald Lloyd, was standing on our driveway and I ran straight into his arms, clinging tightly to him. I grabbed hold of his leg like a drowning boy clutching at a life raft. Did he realise how serious my situation was?

He must have known it was severe. I had always been too scared to meet his gaze before. I remembered thinking back to those finger-wagging lectures about his fragile grass as he led me across his garden to his front door. Pointing me away from the scene, he asked if I was okay and what had happened all in the same question. Dazed, I barely shook my head. Had I answered his question? I couldn't be sure.

I sat at the dining table of his living room, aware of my surroundings but still lost in a trance. I tried my best to block out the noise coming from just the other side of the wall separating our houses and the two different worlds right now. I remember scanning the room, searching for a distraction.

Donald's room, the same shape and size as ours but configured so differently. It was separated into four different living spaces even though he lived alone. In one corner, where my toys were stacked high, stood an imposing dark rosewood

6

grandfather clock surrounded by old paintings of ships. Parallel to this was an old wooden writing desk with matching chair and purposed desk lamp, a floor to ceiling bookcase full of hardback volumes, and then finally a small TV with single armchair facing.

I sat at the dining table all afternoon, not wanting anything from the many people that approached me, all speaking in hushed tones, some in uniform. It became a badge of honour, telling people I was fine. It was dark outside when my mum and dad sat down in front of me, adopting the same hushed tone as all those before, and told me my brother was dead.

Chapter Three – Jimmy's funeral

The days that followed were long. I hardly spoke, nobody did. The church was full, the whole village in attendance and most of Jimmy's school. They were grouped for the service, their red school jumpers with black ties gave the visual impression of an overflowing poppy field in the church. As the coffin was carried into the church, everybody bowed their heads, some out of respect, and others said afterwards they were too afraid to watch. I stood at the pew looking around the church, feeling rebellious for not bowing my head. I watched my mum bury her head into my dad like before; he held her tight.

Although I was only 11-years-old, the funeral was the third I had attended following the passing of my grandparents the previous year. This one was different. For my grandparents, speech after speech detailed their lives, the places they had visited, their many achievements, and the families who grew up around them. Yet for Jimmy, my dad spoke only about how he would be missed and what he had not achieved, how his 14-year-old son would not be coming home for his favourite tea of bangers and mash. He would not be playing football on Saturday with the team. He would not be going to college. He would not be enjoying his first pint in the pub. He would not be travelling around the world sending back postcards for the fridge. He would not be bringing a girl home to our sleepy village and showing her his first school or where he snuck his first cigarette. My dad spoke about how Jimmy had been so cruelly taken from us in the prime of his life.

I didn't understand, he'd not been kidnapped. He had killed himself. The screams I heard on 19th February 1986 were my parents discovering his body hanging from the joists in the garage. Nobody had told me this at the time, but I heard my mum talking on the phone in the same hushed tone, and I heard others saying similar in the days leading up to the funeral. My lasting memory of the day was silly. I counted how many people approached my mum and dad after the service and simply saying 'let me know if there is anything I can do?' I counted 18.

As the colder weather began tailing off in the weeks that followed, so did the visitors. Nobody had to pretend anymore. I would listen to my mum crying in Jimmy's room for hours at a time. I was helpless, unable to comprehend it all. His bedroom door remained shut, only my mum was allowed in. It became her shrine.

My dad had massive mood swings, and it scared me. We could be in the car and all of a sudden he would swear at the top of his voice, banging his fist on the steering wheel, speeding after someone as if in a car chase. Other times he would disappear, sometimes for days, my mum wouldn't know his whereabouts and didn't care. Then out of the blue, he would give me presents and gobble me up with his big outstretched arms and hold me, telling me how much he loved me, tears filling his eyes. I learned to tiptoe around him.

Months passed before my dad paid attention to his appearance and returned to work. I was back at school, and mum finally started talking about something other than Jimmy or the funeral. We even managed a holiday in Brixham, my mum inviting my best friend Davy, filling the empty chair staring back at us at dinner time. It took a special effort from all of us to maintain a veneer of normality.

My parents got me a bunk bed so I could have friends over to stay most weekends. They even bought me a television. I was the only one of my friends to have this, which meant spending more time in my room, but I think that suited everyone. We still did activities as a family of three, but it always felt a little forced. Days spent planning for a picnic, a trip to the seaside next month, and everything put on the calendar like a binding contract.

The school became a minefield of piercing reminders that would invariably cause distress for my mum and dad. I re-member the parents evening in my first year at Baysworth Secondary, the same school Jimmy had attended. They were rushing to meet with my teachers in the assembly hall when they both stopped suddenly and stared at the trophy cabinet, a picture of the U15 County Cup Winners 1985 with a grinning Jimmy standing centre of the back row. My mum reached for my dad's hand and did not let go throughout the rest of the evening. Every other parent was being dragged around to each teacher station gripping in one hand a cup of coffee in a polystyrene cup, a rolled-up timetable in the other. My mum and dad ambled at their own pace, in perfect unison, having a private grieve amongst the first-year pupils, parents, and teaching staff.

Some occasions seemed more poignant than others, Jimmy's birthday, the 19th February each year, Christmas and New Year. I grew accustomed to these occasions being unpredictable, sombre, tearful, and occasionally hostile, all on the same day.

On my 14th birthday, things took a more dramatic turn. I was excited about my party, we hired a clown and organised games, and I had my entire class coming. The first time I sensed all was not well was finding my parents in the living room talking with the door closed. The door was never closed. I walked in, and they stopped talking abruptly, staring at the black screen of the television from their seat on the sofa. I was immediately sent away. I returned an hour or so later to find them in the same position, but this time I was sent to my room. The phone started ringing with a frequency I had never heard before, each time my mum answering, and the return of her hushed tone. One by one, my friend's parents apologetically arrived to drop them off for the party. Either they noticed the lack of decorations or they knew somehow my parents had not left the living room all morning.

It was my parents who were centre of attention on my birthday. In the end, only half of my class came. The clown did some funny tricks, but there were no games, all the parents confined themselves to the kitchen with my mum and dad. We opened our goody bags and finished them off before the cake. I blew out my candles. There were no photographs and an hour after the party started, my party was over.

The house was full of tension for the rest of the summer holidays. Two days before I was due back at school, my parents sat me down in the kitchen and told me I would not be returning to Baysworth Secondary. My mum was going to live with her sister for a short time in Chichester, a couple of hours away, and I would be living with them too. There was a good school with my place already secured to start in a few days. It was a lot to take in. Instead of telling me one reason (maybe the truth), my mum threw lots of reasons at me, looking to the ceiling as if reciting her script, hoping one would resonate.

She said *Baysworth secondary was undergoing renovation and rather than delay the start of the year they thought it better I changed schools...*

Auntie needs looking after, and I'm the only family she has...

Auntie has a dog. You can take him for walks and have a four-legged friend...

Chichester is a lovely place...

There is little work around at the moment, so your Dad has to stay in Baysworth...

I remember it must have worked. With so many motives, I put up little resistance, I always played the numbers game, and they knew this. Five reasons why I should eat my vegetables? Three reasons why we cannot watch this film? Four reasons why I deserve more pocket money.

I mumbled something as a half-hearted objection about dad not coming with us. '*This doesn't change anything,*' my mum responded. It changed everything.

Maybe all were true, but none were the reason we were moving to Chichester, and I knew it would not be for a short time.

Chapter Four - Returning 'Home'

As I drove the final few miles to Baysworth, the guilt of not visiting my father at home in his final years began to fade. It had been a punishing 8-hour drive from Glasgow. Leaving the deserted city streets, the roads wider and tower blocks taller so early in the morning, devoid of its people, devoid of its pulse. I was loaded with four boxes sitting on my back seat and a suitcase in the boot, all my possessions comfortably fitting in my old Ford Focus. Hours upon hours hugging the dirty grey barrier on the motorway that runs the length of the country, the grey skies a reflection of the monochrome patchwork road, lined by a shiny border of tar. The only sound being the monotonous drone of the tyres on the road.

After finally turning off the conveyer belt of motorways, I had to navigate the windy, unforgiving bends of the Dorset countryside with sunlight fading. They were much busier all these years later. The tractors and old army green Land Rovers being replaced by big powerful 4x4's hurtling round the hidden bends as if on a Scalextric track.

The single pleasure of my early visits to my dad's had been the quiet country roads, an hour door to door from Chichester, allowing time for contemplation. After moving North to Glasgow, the slog of the motorways was far less appealing, but by then, so was spending time with dad.

As I turned onto the high street, I realised, willing or not, Baysworth had conformed to consumerism with monolithic retailers placed where family favourites had stood for generations. I slowed down as I passed where Baysworth Bakery once stood, remembering Mrs Fothergill's generous smile with every freshly baked scone. The scent of flower and warming butter flooded my mind's eye, and I could picture the afternoon sunlight sneaking underneath the awning, causing the sugared pastries to glitter like gold. In its place, submerged into new-build flats was the latest Subway outlet, selling sandwiches by reference number with discarded plastic wrappers swirling on the footpath outside, only coming to rest as it lodged into an abandoned coke can.

As I continued through the High Street, I caught sight of the stone carving, the old fashioned carving of the village crest that recalled some other generation. I'd hoped to see the familiar red, white and green table cloths of Luigi's family Italian, but in its place was Domino's Pizza. '*Domino's Pizza,*' I said allowed, scoffing. The double-fronted glass windows covered in loud pictures advertising the latest two-for-one deals with garish bubble writing, more akin to the home-made sign announcing the village jumble sale. Where we once stood in line waiting for our table, there was now delivery drivers awaiting instruction, using their motorbike helmets to prop their heads against the wall. Neon lights of vape shops commanded attention, where once stood Bennets Ironmongers and the wistful image of Mr Bennet standing by the door in his brown overalls. My spirits mourned the loss of the village I had once known.

My dad would have hated this change. He would have ranted for hours, '*it's just not the same,*' his familiar moan, I could hear him now, although I would never hear his voice again. I never gave him a chance.

In a village like Baysworth, I half-expected the old Woolworths to be there still. A trip to Woolworths was the weekend entertainment. On entering Mum would always turn right to the clothes. You could determine a child's age just by where they shopped in the store. Younger ones at the front for all the toys, a few years later advancing to the middle of the store to pick n 'mix sweets. The older kids to the back for computer games, videos, and sports equipment. That's where I always found Jimmy.

I had hoped the old video rental shop would still be there, assuming a reluctant expansion to DVD and Blue-Ray was enough to render Netflix obsolete in this little forgotten corner of Dorset. It once represented our pre-lude to the weekend but now was a charity shop, ironically probably stacked full of DVDs nobody wanted, and it was one of six I counted in the High Street. And coffee shops, coffee shops everywhere.

All these mass-market signs and names had the presence of soulless tombstones, rendering my childhood buried without so much an epitaph to remind coming generations of their existence and close-knit community. The sad reality is I could have been driving through any town in the UK rather than my home village of Baysworth. It was not just the springing up of monotone flats or the blah high street chains; the people seemed to have changed also. Everybody had a purposeful stride, somewhere to go. I remember how tiresome walking through the High Street used to be, with Mum stopping and talking to every other person, that's how you learned what was going on and who it was going on with.

The road junctions were littered with traffic lights, no longer trusting local knowledge and goodwill, with narrow roads not fit for the invasion of the proclaimed Chelsea tractors.

As I drove out of the High Street, it appeared in front of me. An immediate lump in my throat as I saw the school standing on top of the hill and I sub-consciously slowed down. A hill we once walked up, sometimes eight abreast shoving whoever was at the end into the bushes every 50 yards despite promises to stop. The same hill we ran down at the sound of the bell to secure the back seat on the bus home, ties undone and wrapped around our wrist, bag slung over one shoulder and a tennis ball being kicked until it ran off down the main road turning heads and stopping traffic along the way.

I kept the same slow pace for the remaining miles to Dad's, out of both curiosity in case I missed something and subconsciously delaying my pending arrival. On either side of the road, sprawling new homes the size of castles hid behind iron gates. Flash cars parked in front of detached garages. Each dwelling separated by acres of land, with trampolines and quad bikes sitting proudly on manicured gardens where farm animals once roamed. Baysworth may still be set in the countryside, but it was no longer rural.

I turned off the deserted Quartermile Road into Hatch End. The road was narrow and darkened by the hour, under the spell of the enormous Maple trees—a solitary street light signalling halfway before reaching the six houses making up Hatch End. Three similar-looking properties, generous in size, split to form semi-detached houses. As I drove past the first two prominent imposing properties, I wondered and doubted at the same time if the occupants were the same as my childhood as I roll-called their names in my head. I slowed to a snail's pace as I went past Roger and Mary Knight's house. It looked in excellent condition, newly painted, immaculate garden, many a weekend spent on it I am sure. The final two properties could not have been more contrasting. My dad's house stood in complete darkness, devoid of life and appeared to be retreating into the growth of the bushes and ivy around it, a ghostly silhouette of its former self. Donald's house seemed double the size, beaming with colour and life.

My lights stared down the driveway, which looked unfamiliarly long without the old Volvo parked halfway down. Even the old tow that sat dormant for years with a constant puddle of water on its cover and moss growing on the wheels had gone. For some reason, I could not help wonder where it had gone, and who had moved it. Dad had never mentioned it. The road ends here, and Baysworth woods start. I remember my dad standing in the lounge cursing under his breath as another car would pull up on our drive, only to reverse and complete their U-turn. Lost or just nosey bastards. He once put up a *'no turning'* sign up in the garden, but mum rationally protested what was that going to achieve, if you reached this far you had no choice but to turn, we were the dead end.

I walked around the perimeter of the house to stretch my legs more than from curiosity, further delaying turning the key. As I walked around the front through the overgrown vines, my eyes met with Donald Lloyd next door, standing in his lounge. I was about to raise a wave when his arms stretched out, grabbing both ends of curtain and pulling them shut. I stood at my dad's front door, took a deep breath and turned the key.

The chill hit me as I pushed open the door, colder than outside. The smell was earthy, almost moss-like, probably from all the shoes of the visiting authorities, my dad would have hated that, '*shoes off at the door.*' The living room was a mess. Old

17

newspapers all over the table, spilling onto the floor below, letters resting on top of the envelopes, tea-stained cups, an old plate with remains of a blackened dinner caked onto the knife and fork resting on the arm of his chair, a disregarded disposable plastic dish still with half of the contents to the side and of course a whiskey bottle at the foot of his chair. I crouched on the floor to clear away some of the empty cans, looking down on me, the three horse racing paintings my mum hated. Nijinsky, Dancing Brave, and Shergar, three classic winners back in their day. He used to wax lyrical about them, but mum was more concerned that he spent a fortune buying them at auction. I went from room to room checking for life, silence answering me. The kitchen tops full of stains and crumbs, the bin overflowing, sink full of dirty dishes and finding more bird food in the cupboard than actual provisions, I wondered what his diet was like in his final months.

The abandoned state continued throughout the house, and I felt more than a pang of guilt. He had not been coping. I remember him once furious with Jimmy for leaving the milk out, throwing it into the fridge and slamming the door shut causing its entire contents to rattle. He once threw a cup against the kitchen wall saying he was sick of staring at it sitting on the breakfast table, and would empty the cutlery tray into the sink if he thought the knives had crossed into the spoons. Had he just given up or not noticed in his final days?

I took another deep breath, almost symbolically, as I grabbed the door handle leading to the garage. It was locked. I walked round the front, to the big metal brown garage door, also locked. I went back to my car and carried in my suitcase from the boot; the boxes could wait until morning. I picked up the half bottle of whisky from the floor, rinsed a glass and poured myself a generous measure. I swirled the amber liquid. It stuck to the side of the glass as it rotated. I raised it to my lips, the piercing smell alerting my senses, the sharp taste bitter and sweet as one, followed by burning at the back of my throat: pleasure and pain, a drink defining life itself. I paused, no thoughts reaching me, before sipping again, closing the loop on my brain.

I sat for hours in the darkened room before staggering up the stairs holding the remains of the bottle in my glass. I paused at the top. A personal crossroad. I had not given it any thought until now on which room I would sleep. My dad's bedroom was a mess with sheets gathered at the foot of the bed, and my old bedroom was filled with junk. This only left me with Jimmy's old room. As I sat on his bed, I raised my glass of whisky above my head and gave a silent toast. Tomorrow would be a long day, the looming funeral. Sleep would come easy that evening; the whisky helped.

I awoke groggily. My confusion lasted more than the usual morning disorientation. Wondering if I was still dreaming, I was surrounded by everything foreign except for the familiar and sweet taste of sugar from the whiskey coated to my dry mouth. I tasted it all over again, but stale this time making me dry cough. My lungs expanded slowly as the mist in my brain began to clear. My head ached, but the feeling of regret long gone. I was surrounded by the smell of staleness from the pillow and bedsheets that I hadn't noticed the night before, and the scent clung to my clothing and skin. I sat up and took in my surroundings as if for the first time. Jimmy's room. Jimmy's bedroom but nothing of Jimmy, nothing of anything.

There was a rustling outside. I opened the curtain to see Donald in his shed, its door open. I pictured Jimmy, helping him as he often did; mum called it his second home. If Jimmy was not in his room, he was in Donald's shed repairing a hinge or sawing wood for his latest carpentry project. He would have sat at this window and seen Donald in his shed as I did that morning and darted down to join him. I got dressed with slightly less vigour and went out to say hello to Donald, hoping to explain it was me who arrived at the house late last night.

He looked up to find me standing in front of him. He had seen me last night, he had been expecting me to return for the funeral and in his words, '*see to the house.*' He asked where I was living these days, and if I have a family of my own, both questions caused me to hesitate, both were difficult for me to answer. *Had my dad never spoken about me?* He did not pass on the standard condolences for my dad even though they had been neighbours for decades. *Was he that bitter about the state of the garden?* Donald was a proud man, with some arrogance at best and a sense of entitlement at worst. I always had the impression he talked down to our family while commanding the respect of others. I began walking away, but stopped short and turned again, like the trademark of my favourite TV Detective Columbo from the 1970's American TV show.

'*I'll fix up the garden,*' I said, desperately wanting to patch up whatever bad feelings may have been lingering. '*If there is anything I can do while I'm here, please let me know.*'

A heavy silence hung in the air between us, as Donald looked me in the eye for the first time, his face screwed. '*But what can you do,*' he replied, without inflexion to make to a question. If it wasn't a question, it left me without the possibility of responding with any sort of gesture. Donald returned to his shed and shut the door.

I had no time to dwell on this strange reunion. I had a funeral to attend.

Chapter Five – the present, 1 day after the funeral

I have a thumping headache, the pain throbbing so hard I expect it to break through my skull. My mouth is dry. The back of my neck is damp with sweat, and I reach back to feel my shirt collar rubbing at it. I look down and see my black shoes standing to attention on my feet, trousers with one leg pulled up just below my knee. I am so thirsty. I sit up on the sofa I passed out on and squint at the bright light coming through the window. I kick off my shoes, my black cotton socks creased where they had been squashed with sweat stains. I feel a momentary relief, my feet free from their shackles. I pull at my shirt from its twisted state within my belt, the cold buckle pressing into my bare stomach, leaving a red crease on my skin. I undo another button on my shirt, freeing the collar from my damp neck. I have a nagging feeling weaving through my mind. Something is not right.

My mind begins to playback the events of yesterday, of course, my dad's funeral. I remember standing at the pulpit delivering the eulogy. I remember all those grey faces telling what a lovely service it was. I remember the sandwiches not being ready as we entered the pub and I remember having quite a few beers. The chicken wings were spicy, and I remember wanting to be anywhere else, I remember staying late, talking with some pub regulars about nothing, I remember an argument, some shouting, I feel disturbed. I feel guilt. I want to close my eyes and wake up again.

On the coffee table are hamburger wrappers, some empty beer cans, and a wine bottle, five centimetres of red wine resting at the bottom. I allow myself a smirk, a momentary release from the self-loathing, at least I did not finish the bottle, and I would have thought the same last night as well, thinking I was smart. Like a weight crashing to the floor the realisation they came from the petrol station. I drove there after the pub, after six hours in the pub. Stupid man. *Boom*, a second weight crashing to the floor, a flashback of an argument with the cashier in the petrol station. I hope I did not do anything stupid. There would have been cameras everywhere. I still do not feel at ease despite my vague recollections, something else tucked in the back of my consciousness, tugging away but still hidden.

I press the cool rim of the glass against my cracked lips. I chew the water, forcing it down my throbbing, burning throat. I replay the mundane conversations from yesterday. One man, Terry I think was his name, told me my dad would be missed around the church and how his volunteering was much appreciated. I remember smiling and thinking *this man must be confused.* People dig deep to compliment the deceased. I think hard, I can't recall dad mentioning the church, he did not even attend when we were on stage at the Harvest festival, but then I cannot remember him attending any school performance.

A lady called Elsa talked about how my dad had helped her son during his darkest times. Reg and Anna from the bowling club said something similar about their son, how my dad had been a regular visitor to the children's home in Teyford. I should have

22

paid more attention, asked more questions, but my mind had been focused on the bottom of my pint glass.

My concern back to the coffee table and near-empty wine bottle. It would have been obvious I was drunk when I pulled up at the garage, probably why I argued with the cashier, did I even pay? Could I be arrested for theft and driving under the influence? I pull out my wallet from my suit trousers, a receipt for a microwave burger box, four cans of lager and a bottle of wine, thank goodness. Although the cameras I am sure would have captured my incriminating stumble back to my car. The police could come around at any time and breathalyse me, and I would still be over the limit. There were plenty of witnesses to confirm my daytime drinking.

I drink more water, force down some toast and scrub my teeth and tongue clean. I feel paranoid. For the rest of today, I will stay in the house, too embarrassed to go out, an all too familiar feeling.

I continue to playback the events from the petrol station. I am confident we left on good terms, I remember waving, and we may even have known each other from school. It wasn't the petrol station.

Caroline.

Oh shit. I pick up my phone and staring back at me is a message 'DO NOT CALL ME ANYMORE' timed at 20.40 last night. The guilt cuts into my gut, turning over and over my insides.

I look at my call log, 18 attempted calls to Caroline, all unanswered. My eyes are drawn to the one connected call at 20.33 just 3 min 47 seconds in duration but enough it seems to ignite a firework.

Shame washes over me. I had all these notions of being a

better husband during separation. She would have known I was drunk before answering the phone. She would have tried to help. I probably put some sort of blame on her, she hates that. I hate that. She used to call me a frightened child, recognising my fear trigger as anything emotional, as my body continues to adopt the fight or flight. I long for the day to expand on these two narrowest of routes.

Chapter Six – 2 days after

I lie awake, hoping that sleep will come. I recheck my watch. Too much going through my head, Caroline, my shopping list, Caroline, where should I start on the garden, Caroline.

The text message sits in my hand like a glass shard, the tighter I cling to it the deeper it cuts me.

I pray sleep will come.

Chapter Seven – 3 days after

I lie on my brother's bed and visualise the room as Jimmy's again. Light blue wallpaper peeling at the corners, splattered with blotches of blue tack that had been half picked off. Posters of footballers on the wall, Gary Lineker and Chris Waddle in England shirts. A picture of the Bernabeu stadium with 'Espana 82' and a Spanish flag plastered across the top. Discarded Panini football stickers all over his cupboard door, the club crests of Motherwell and Everton, anonymous moustached footballers, duplicates of his collection already tucked away in his sticker album. I can still smell the glossy magazines sprawled across the floor, copies of 'Shoot' football magazine, the Beano and Dandy mixed in with his schoolbooks. Centre of his dressing table was a big black stereo with speakers either side, cassette tapes sitting on top of the record player.

I loved his room growing up. I envied everything in it and would sometimes just sit on his bed, admiring the heroes around me. A three-year age gap is a lifetime between boy and teenager.

I venture only as far as downstairs and flick through the mail sitting beneath the letterbox. My attention is drawn to one envelope handwritten and addressed to me. My mind goes straight to Caroline, and I hurriedly rip it open. The personal touch, and with that, my excitement is quickly lost as I read an invoice from *'Love R Flowers, always personally delivered'* for £185. I blow the air from my cheeks at the excessive *personal hand delivery charge of £50,* the listed address for the shop is in Bournemouth. There must be a mistake; whoever ordered them should have contacted a local branch. The other letters also look like bills, the non-descript font typed on a template, an account number referenced at the bottom of the address—another thing to sort out, tomorrow maybe, not today.

Chapter Eight – 4 days after

I have been awake since 5 am lying in bed as if caged in a cell. Five hours awake. Nothing running through my mind, although it should be. I still have no plans. I contracted with myself that I would wait until after the funeral, but today, I need to get my dad's paperwork in order. Tomorrow I need to start on the garden and the other abandoned jobs in the house. Next week. Next week I will plan my life.

I promised the solicitor I would drop off the paperwork on Monday concerning my dad's financial affairs to advance the probate. He always kept his business affairs very close to his chest, and I never asked, so this will be like Russian roulette. I have no idea what will come of this, or for that matter where to start. I chose to start with a bottle of red, it is after lunchtime I justify, although I have not had lunch.

I stand the bottle of Pinot Noir with a crystal glass on the dining room table and open up the cardboard box marked 'important'. It is a healthy pile, needing two hands to lift, my thumb stretched over the top to keep them in the order they were filed. I pour myself a glass of red, my fuel, and flick through the pile. I find a collection of bank statements, receipts, guarantees for electrical goods and some old postcards.

A separate mini pile commands my attention. It receipts

of bookings and cleaning bills held together by a paperclip from our holidays in Devon. Regardless of the time of year, we went to the same holiday cottage in Brixham, we may have had part-ownership of it. My dad was meticulous about keeping paperwork as he did not trust the management company. I need not have worried too much about the weight of my task as sandwiched between various papers is a car manual, instructions for the washing machine and an old school yearbook, taking these three out more than halves the size of my task.

The school yearbook is Baysworth Secondary 1984/85, two years before Jimmy died. I pour myself another glass and brace myself for a flood of memories. After all these years, I do not have a picture of Jimmy to call my own. When my mum passed away, I included her two photographs of him amongst her most treasured belongings to be in her possession at the time of cremation. It felt right as she continued to mourn for him right up to her passing. *'No parent should have to bury their child'* became her mantra. It defined her. Her life was without purpose. I simply accepted it, but looking back, with life experience and maturity of my own, I feel a fresh bitterness. She gave up on my life too. Our conversations were merely functional, no emotion or thought.

I flick through the yearbook and spot him instantly. Jimmy stands in the middle row behind seated classmates, in front of others standing on benches, he is four from the left, one from the centre. The bright red sweaters match their radiating, innocent smiles and rosy cheeks on show. None of the class appears to be the same height as another, and it's mostly the girls that stand tallest on the back row. Jimmy's smile is featured throughout the book, the football and cricket team photo, and back of the coach on a school trip.

At the end of the yearbook amongst the adverts for sheds, local trades, and taxis are other photographs slipped in between the last page and cover. I take the picture out for a better look. It is framed in a bendy cheap cardboard with the words 'Final year students, 1985/86.' I imagine the photo being taken in autumn, just in time to purchase for Christmas gifts for grandparents. Jimmy is stood on the back row, far right, with a wider gap than necessary between him and the person next to him. He looks so much older with floppy unkempt hair covering much of his face which is littered with spots. Gone is the beaming smile, rosy cheeks, and sparkle in his eyes. He looks stern and void of interest. The difference a year makes, the effect exams can have.

I pull out the next document, a statement from Dorset Police. The text is a horrible dark green ink printed on fine paper that has been crumpled over the years. It is an official warning against my dad for his reported behaviour towards Mr Donald Lloyd of number 5, Hatch End. Also, is a reminder that verbal abuse and threatening behaviour is criminal behaviour resulting in prosecution if repeated, the statement is dated December 1998.

I read the letter a further three times, perplexed that my dad would go this far and wonder what could have prompted it to go beyond his mumbling complaints at the dinner table. I set the police warning on a separate pile and continue to read receipts for a car MOT, a lawnmower, a credit card statement, and then I reach three newspaper cuttings. I only catch sight of half the headline before I drop them to the floor, myself wanting to follow. I hold myself upright on the table, arms stretched wide, fingers gripping, and heart accelerating. I look down at my feet and read the headline. I need a drink.

Chapter Nine – 4 days after

I stare at the words in front of me, willing for them to scramble across the page to make different words like a cartoon. A picture of the school I have seen a thousand times. A bigger font and bolder colour than any newspaper headline I have seen before, reading '**Sexual Abuse Scandal at Baysworth School.**' It was a headline more fitting for a Sunday tabloid paper than our local rag, which is more akin to reporting traffic congestion or a lost cat. I read the article in disbelief, of how police are investigating serious allegations of sexual abuse against pupils by the teachers going back four years. I cannot think why my dad would have kept this amongst his documents. I scan it again looking for clues. My eyes are drawn to the date of the paper, 19th July 1989, the year Jimmy died, and the same day as my 14th birthday party.

I think back to how the mood not so much swung in our house that day, but more fell off a cliff. One moment we were blowing up balloons and making sandwiches, and the next my mum and dad were disappearing into the living room, speaking in hushed voices. Hushed voices between them became the new normal from that day on. The phone ringing all morning. My friends were dropped off apologetically by their parents, who all huddled in the kitchen, and how the party was never really a party. I can only imagine how these conversations went. This disturbing headline put all those apologies, diverted glances, and hushed conversations into a new perspective. Parents must have speculated on the teachers, swapped suspicions, added dark elements to the rumours, and made the victim's agony even more sinister.

The victims. *Jimmy?*

They must have all thought it, explaining the focus on my mum and dad and not the parents of Davy Thompson, Laurie James, or Nathan Bryson that day. The focus was on the parents of Jimmy Jenkins. The guilt consumes me. I remember feeling so hard done by, I sulked for days, I thought they did not care about me, but how could they? The headline consumed their focus, and I was a bystander, my party a blur.

Jimmy took his own life on a Wednesday morning, the middle of the week, dressed in his school uniform. Rather than walk to the school bus that day, he walked into our garage, took the rope from the trailer and tied it to the beam on the garage ceiling and stepped onto the wooden stool. The ultimate, permanent escape from what must have been the most frightening alternative, going to school that day. For the first time, I had a possible glimpse, a suggestion into just how terrifying the alternative was. I have spent 30 years speculating and imagining what this might have been. I'm drunk on emotion, flirting between anger and sympathy to Jimmy, intensified by the explosive shock and sustained by the alcohol.

A second paper is tucked underneath, dated a couple of days later and reports how the probe was started after police received complaints from concerned parents, and how the school denied all accusations but were cooperating with the investigation. There is a hotline number published on the front page for worried parents or those with further information. This is so personal to my family and me, but of course, without addressing us by name. I don't know if I feel relieved or bitter. I want more information, I want details, and I want to know how it ends. I scramble to the bottom of the box, no more newspapers, just more receipts. The probate can wait, I need to find out what happened at the school, and I know just where to start.

Chapter Ten – 5 days after

'You go, it's your turn.'

'But you kicked it over.'

We spent as much time arguing as we did playing football. Whose turn was it in goal, who kicked it too hard, no volleys allowed, but the longest disputes were always who had to retrieve the ball after it flew over the fence into our neighbour's back garden. I would walk around the front keeping to the path, ring the doorbell and wait the agonising minutes before Mr Lloyd opened the door and stared down at me, braced for his lecture. I would plead forgiveness before he would reluctantly toss the ball over the fence, vowing to keep it next time. The next time was also my turn. Even in those days as young boys, living without fear, we were scared of Mr Lloyd. He was a man of intimidating stature; he was the History teacher before eventually becoming Headmaster at Baysworth Secondary. He dressed as a teacher even at weekends, always with sharp coffee breath and was quick to scold us for making too much noise or running over his precious garden which offered a vital two-second short cut to our front door. He carried with him a sense of entitlement like he was forever judging others and particularly us.

My dad and Donald would have been similar ages, neighbours

in symmetrical semi-detached houses but from very different stock. Donald was the typical ex-army type, and when I was younger, I thought he spoke like a king, even today he would not sound out of place making public service announcements on behalf of the Royal family. He is a tall man, walks with pride, a straight back and chest out with combed grey hair. Most conversations would reference to his army days or a historical battle, most of which went over our heads. He was always trying to educate us on apartheid or communism, when all I knew was Nintendo and Subbuteo.

My dad was highly suspicious of him, likely grown out of jealousy as Jimmy got on well with Donald. Jimmy developed a real passion for History when he moved to Secondary school, and he loved all of Donald's war stories, reading his books and looking at old photographs.

At the dinner table, Jimmy would talk about the Cold War or Battle of Leningrad, much to dad's annoyance. His frustrations grew louder as Jimmy spent more and more time at Donald's, learning how to use his tools, learning DIY and woodwork. It got to the point on weekends that when tea was ready, I had to go and shout Jimmy to come in from the garden, knowing he would be sawing or mending something in Donald's shed. Dad used to say that was what the Yellow Pages were for, but mum always encouraged it, *'he should know DIY and let's face it, you're not going to teach him.'*

I remember a time when Dad and Donald were friends. He would come over for drinks on a Sunday afternoon, and mum would cook an extra pie for him from time to time feeling sorry for him living on his own, which Donald was always quick to point out was by choice. Both were Rotary club members, and Dad even talked about joining the Masons at one time. He petitioned the local club with a nomination and an endorsement from Donald, only to be 'blackballed' by the other members. Dad was furious. He reacted with typical spite, mimicking Donald's hosted annual drinks party and his association with the world's most well-known secret society.

I remember dad dismissing the Freemasons as *'Nothing more than an 18th-century boys club who dress up in funny aprons and have a stupid handshake.'* Jimmy did little to appease this by telling my dad that *'some of history's most authoritative figures were Masons, including Winston Churchill, Benjamin Franklin, and George Washington.'* My dad winced, knowing the source of this information before replying *'add to your list the KFC man, hardly an authority figure.'* Jimmy was quick to joke *'he was still a Colonel.'* I remember it well as I was in awe of Jimmy, standing up to dad for the first time, a coming of age for him to show his intellect and growing confidence.

Dad would always be moaning under his breath, for all to hear, about the noise of his TV coming through the walls. Sometimes it was about his hedge cuttings that fell on our lawn or his car parked on our side of the shared drive. The complaints were of the same nature, born from suspicion and jealousy.

And now, with the newspaper in my hand, my resolve is pumped up to march over to Donald Lloyd's door to demand answers. He was a teacher during this time and was appointed Headmaster soon after. He would have known everything, the names of who was involved, both victims and staff. The time that has passed will be no excuse; this type of scandal would live long in the memory for a small local comprehensive school like Baysworth.

I slam my door shut and march over the driveway staring at his front door, squeezing the newspaper tightly in my hand, my grenade. The voice in my head is angry but also struggling to put words together. My pace slowing involuntarily as my mind computes, my eyes fixed on the door that opens in front of me.

'Ah Philip, were you were coming to see me, I am on my way out.' He stands tall with a half-smile, his body facing me, but his eyes and attention focus on his keys.

The mist in my mind suddenly clears. Donald will know that I know very little. I am hearing about it for the first time nearly 30 years on. He could just as easily deflect this away from his old teacher pals.

'Well, are you wanting me or not?' He impatiently demands, standing at his car door now. The heat in my blood and the angry voices return.

'Did you and Dad fall out, and what was it about?'

'Are you asking me or telling me Philip, I am confused by your double-barrelled question?'

'What? Just tell me what happened Donald?'

The last traces of his smile vanish. 'I suggest you focus on your own affairs,' jabbing his finger towards my Dad's house.

I stand rooted to the spot watching his car accelerate out of sight. The anger flares again inside me, *why did I let him dismiss me so easily?*

I am still holding the newspaper article in my hand. I think back to the teachers at the time, back to my own time at Baysworth Secondary. I can picture faces and recall names, but my memory is too vague and distorted to point any fingers. I will need more information before confronting Donald properly, prove to him I know enough not to be dismissed. And what did he mean by looking closer to home? Can he be so upset at some overgrown weeds and flaking paint?

I need more information and try another internet search for some answers on the Police investigation, but find nothing. I will need an old school approach to this. My first destination tomorrow will be the library to go through the archives of the local papers and find out how this ended. I am hungry for the first time in a long time and order a pizza, knowing I will be over the limit if I were to get in my car. I vow never to do that again, not here in Baysworth, and I have too much to do, too many people depending on me.

Chapter Eleven – 6 days after

The newspaper headline consumes my every waking thought, running through the many permutations. As I prepare for my day it dominates the room, luring me in, taunting me. My body tenses each time I catch sight of it, I need answers.

As I sit in my car, I realise this is the first time I have been out of the house since the funeral, nearly a week ago. Nobody has called at the house, nobody has telephoned. I have not spoken to anybody in almost a week.

I am at the door of the library as they open. Entering in single file through the heavy swing door, I am in unfamiliar territory, a lost soul as others take up their position, knowing their place. An elderly man dressed in a blazer clutching his sandwich wrapped in cling film sits down at a table full of newspapers, two ladies of a similar vintage clutching a flask amble towards the fiction. A couple of students plug in laptops, and a teacher herds a chain of young school kids to a children's corner.

An assistant asks me what publications I want to reference and advises my best bet would be the archive machine rather than searching the shelves. I take a seat at an old monitor, as deep as it was wide, and a dirty sun stained off-white colour. I squint trying to read the poorly scanned copies on the archaic machine boasting the same pixels of an old Nokia phone. I wrestle with the curser as it is ultra-sensitive, accelerating me months rather than next day publications. I eventually land on 19th July 1989 and recognise the paper image from the one I had in my hand only yesterday. I read through the article again as if doubting my state of mind from yesterday. Carefully, I pull the curser down half an inch to reveal the following day's paper which I also recognise from the pile in the box, and it is dated 21st July 1989 accepting they did not publish on a Sunday.

My appetite growing as the story continues from Saturday to Monday thus far. I pull down, hungry for the next instalment. I stare hard at the headline about a new bypass proposed for the area, dated 23rd July 1989, flicking to the following day and more on the bypass plans, next day is the same and same after that. Where is my story? I bang my fist on the table. I flick through further but jump far too many dates, punished for my heavy touch. I stand up and take a couple of steps back, taking in my surroundings for the first time. Much busier now, heads bowed and lost in different world's. A muffled stillness with each figure distancing from the next, possessions spread out marking territory. Each rustle of a plastic bag piercing the hushed silence.

I wipe my hands across my shirt and settle in my plastic chair, the quietness and peace of the room infectious. My eyes squint once again to the monitor and the reference to *my story* dated 6th August 1989. Wedged against an article about the adverse weather condition in the County, are two paragraphs in a small font with the title '*School investigation closed*'. It concludes with a quote from the investigating officer DI Peter Mayne stating, '*after a thorough investigation I am pleased to say that we have concluded that there is no evidence to back up the allegations made against the school and its employees of any misconduct towards pupils. We thank Baysworth school for their cooperation with our investigation and apologise for any distress or inconvenience caused.'*

My heart sinks, the air sucked out of me. I read it over and over again. This cannot be right, a couple of weeks is not enough time to do a thorough investigation, it was summer holidays and they would not have had time to speak to all the staff and all the pupils. I continue searching, looking for news of the investigation being opened again but find nothing. I feel cheated.

My first thought is to march into the newspaper office, demanding some answers. I change my search to the Nationals but quickly realise there were far more pressing matters nationally at the time. My anger shifts from the newspaper to the police, and so I google 'Detective Inspector Peter Mayne Baysworth.' I read the first entry on the search results and curse out loud, thumping my fist down on the desk, much harder than before. Pain flows up my arm. Heads turn in my direction, eyes staring, heads shaking. I re-read the article. This changes everything.

Chapter Twelve – 6 days after

I cannot trust myself in the outside world. The very reasonable librarian filled me with murderous rage when she rightly asked me to keep the noise down. I pushed some poor guy out the way, his only crime pausing at the door. I shouted at a kid bouncing a ball on the way to school. My anger is spreading throughout my body like a rash as I drive home too fast.

I sit in my car on the driveway of my dad's house needing my deep breaths and look at Donald's house. I open my car door wider than I need to, enough to bang his passenger side door, only able to reach because again he has parked in the middle of our shared driveway. *Bastard.*

A couple more deep breaths give me some control back. I get out of my car and stare at his house; I want him to see me, I want him to wonder why I am staring at him, I want to unnerve him. I scan each window, no sign of movement, probably in his bloody shed. I walk back into my dad's house. What now? My mind suddenly blank, I don't know what to do. I go to the alcohol cabinet by default. I have as good as emptied it over the past week. Drinking an old bottle of peach schnapps would be real desperation. They should have this as a litmus test for defining alcoholics if nothing else in the house would you drink it? The joke is a little too close to home.

I get back in my car and drive to the supermarket, integrating again with everyday life. As I walk around the aisles with my basket for one, I know I am being judged. Microwave meals, a pint of milk, crisps, a crate of London Pride beer, three bottles of wine, a bottle of gin, and four cans of tonic water. I give myself another chuckle thinking back to my favourite comedy sketch of a Harry Enfield character buying groceries. When he got to the checkout, he realises he does not have enough money so puts all the food back leaving him with just two bottles of whiskey at 10 am on a Sunday, the shopkeeper giving a resigned look as if a weekly occurrence. The irony of this sketch is not lost on me. Its 10.37 am.

I purposely ping Donald's car with my door, harder this time, and this time parking much closer to his. A statement made. I leave my shopping bags on the kitchen counter and sit at the dining table. I need a plan, and quick, otherwise I will open a beer, then another, then the wine, ending with me passing out in the afternoon and up all night.

I open my laptop and google again 'Detective Inspector Peter Mayne Baysworth.' I click on the article I read only a couple of hours ago in the library, about how DI Peter Mayne is facing pressure to give up his controversial membership of the freemasons. Commentators claim it is unethical for an investigating officer to be a freemason on the chance a fellow freemason from the same Lodge could be a suspect or critical witness. The article quotes historical cases where such instances occurred.

I read that DI Mayne had not disclosed his freemason membership until he was appointed a senior figure in the local Lodge. In an ongoing attempt to raise the transparency of the freemason membership, the association agreed to publish and list senior figures within their lodges; however, the members of the brotherhood would remain confidential. DI Peter Mayne is listed as one of those senior figures in 1990, although it is believed he had a membership for some time before this allowing time to move up the ranks. By my calculations, it is likely when investigating the Baysworth school allegations that he would have come up against Donald, a member from the same Lodge.

I google 'freemason' to learn more about the world's most well-known secret society. They have a peculiar system of morality with no-one able to define, purpose or reason for their membership. I read about camaraderie, friendship, a sense of belonging, about 'just getting out of the house.'

The personal gain of membership must be more than this, and own favours which may help evade the law, for example, would be enticing for most. The disquiet behind this was rife in the '70s, and '80s. I read extracts from Stephen Knight's book 'Brotherhood' on this very subject, published in 1984. Even in the mid-nineties, the Police Complaints Board could only legislate a voluntary scheme whereby police officers could declare their membership and, by inference, any conflict of interest in their role as a police officer. I cannot believe this, and I reflect on the investigation at the school and imagine the scenario of DI Mayne turning up at the gates, giving a secret handshake to Donald, then drinking together at the Lodge the following week, case closed. The injustice of it all. The injustice to Jimmy, and many more before him. I sit back and take in my surroundings. The light fades outside, and four empty beer cans sit next to me.

I look across to the cabinet at the one picture of my dad in the house, an old one taken maybe about 25 years ago. He stands holding a rucksack, wearing a red waterproof top and big brown boots with heavy laces. He is with two boys aged no more than 14 on what looks like some moors. My dad is dressed for a hike, and the boys are wearing sports tops, tracksuit bottoms and trainers, street trainers, not sports trainers. I stare hard having not noticed the picture before.

'How much did you know dad? How much did you fight this?' I say out loud, and have a flashback to what Roger said in the pub after the funeral. I can picture Roger now in front of me holding a glass of wine in his hand but jabbing with his finger as he told me, *'he lost his fight years ago, that's the real cost of injustice, losing your spirit, your peace, and your ability to sleep at night. The death certificate may say cancer, but that was not the cause.'*

He knew everything, he must have done. I have known for five minutes, and it is killing me inside, my dad knew for years, he fought it and lost. An injustice such as this would have killed bigger men than my dad.

I pace around the house, mumbling under my breath a full rant of me confronting him, all the things I want to say. I feel the anger building up, the toxic mix of being wronged fuelled by alcohol. I need to be smarter than this, stay in control. I will continue to be a good neighbour in his eyes so as not to raise suspicion. I know where this is going, I know where it could lead, but I cannot stop it. It's the proverbial car crash in slow motion. My perpetrator is just 10 yards away from my living room. He is the other side of my wall right now, and he is a sitting duck. The advantage is all mine. I throw a cricket ball against our adjoining wall causing a massive bang, the starting gun for a race. It starts now.

Chapter Thirteen – 7 days after

I lie wide awake once again and tap my phone, lighting up like a beacon, illuminating the whole room and causing me to squint. The clock on my phone says 03.44 and I give a wry smile, precisely two hours since I last checked and I wonder if I will still be wide awake in another two hours. My mind is active, thoughts racing between devising a plan to get the truth and moving quickly to seeking retribution. I so desperately want to confront DI Peter Mayne, to look him in the eye. I imagine going to the Police station first thing in the morning, to speak to the Chief Superintendent, to demand answers. I play out the conversation in my head sitting in his oak-panelled office, drinking tea from a china cup with his assistant taking notes in the corner. Even in my imagination, where you are not always right, but never wrong, I do not know what to say. I think about the newspaper office. They would have the original story archived, the story they couldn't publish. I could demand to see it, quoting freedom of information act or something like that. I go over these plans in my head, selecting what to wear, where to park and factoring in a coffee stop between them.

I wake up again. The last time I looked at my phone, it was 05.07, and I remember lying awake a little after that, so just a couple of hours sleep. The cold light of day paves the way to a more sober, honest appraisal of my plan that was devised under the spell of a trance. The police are unlikely to give me the time of day and I do not want them to alert Donald or give the impression I have a possible grudge to bear. The newspaper is hardly going to grant Joe Public off the street permission to search through their notes for what turned out to be a non-story over 30 years ago.

If I am going to get to the bottom of this, I am going to have to do it myself, and it starts with speaking to my dad's friends. I begin a list. I write down Roger at the top, knowing he is still on holiday, and I have no mobile number for him. Chris Powell is next, but I have not seen or heard of him in years. He was not at the funeral; I am not sure he is even still alive. I sit at the table, twirling my pen.

At times like this, I wish my mum was still alive, or more accurately, I wish we had a different relationship when she was alive. My mum's recovery from Jimmy was slow, one step forward, two steps back. Signs of normality were promptly followed by days of isolation.

Our move to Chichester felt like a surrender rather than a fresh start. My mum was from a generation whereby she expected to be taken care of by her husband. My dad was the sole breadwinner, sorted the bills, owned the family agenda and always the driving—the old fashioned man of the house. In the films, my mum's character would have thrived. All those housewives freed from the shackles, brides from times of austerity who counted the pennies and made the pounds go far. A new lease of life they called it—a chance to re-invent yourself. My mum took time to adjust, a long time, never really learning, just enough to be transactional. She had built her life around the man she married straight out of school and subsequently

47

given up on both, her prime of life forever escaping her.

She hid behind the fact we did not know anybody in a new town, making no effort to socialise. She had a propensity to change the subject if I ever asked about the past. Adopting a '*do not ask, do not tell*' stance, which only fired my curiosity and suspicions at the time. But those suspicions faded as time passed and my mum showed a similar disregard for all things in her life. We never talked about Jimmy's death, we never spoke about the mood swings that followed, and we never spoke about the real reason why we moved to Chichester or why dad just gave up on the both of us. Mum never talked about her job, her day, or her health problems that followed.

I genuinely do not know of anyone else to ask, so I think about those who attended the funeral and scribble down a few names, but that is all they are to me, names. I need to validate them from my hazy, intoxicated memory and then I have to find them. I feel the returning regret for knowing so little about my dad's life, not knowing his friends and knowing so few of those I spoke to at the funeral. Even after his death, rather than learn in retrospect, all I wanted was to be at the bar and lose myself in *my* world. If he didn't have many friends, I should have known before today.

I open my front door and see him at his bin. I raise a smile and wave. Donald does neither but bellows out, 'Hello Philip, how are you?'

Why is he always so formal?

'I am good thank you, Donald, I am just off to the church to tie a few things up from last week.' It is not a lie, I *am* going to the church to re-connect with some of the mourners, but I was also keen to reference the funeral, to see if it sparked a response.

'I am sure you made him proud,'

I want to ask the obvious question of why he did not attend, but I know it would lead to another which would lead to another ending with me firing accusations at him. I need to be calm. I have no cards to show yet.

I pull up to the church car park and walk the wavy old stone path amongst the long grass and gravestones. It is eerily quiet compared to last week. I have arranged to meet the vicar on the proviso of thanking him personally for the service.

'Hello Phil,' he greets me with enthusiasm and an out-stretched hand. He is young for a vicar, more youthful than those you see on TV dramas. His dark hair is scruffy on top, sporting trendy square glasses, dressed in a black shirt and dark jeans. The demanded modern image of the oldest of establishments.

'Good morning vicar,' I reply, my fixed on the pulpit over his shoulder.

'I know you do not feel particularly at home here, so I thought better to have a cup of tea in my office at the back.' He must have noticed my confused look at the mention of office. 'Yes, I have an office, we have more administration, more paperwork, more finances and more marketing material than most companies in Baysworth, and besides where else would we store our props, come, follow me.'

I like the vicar; he comes across as very humble without being false. I thank him for the service, and we have some small talk about the weather and the organ which was off timing for the second hymn.

'I was hoping you could help me vicar. I am looking to engage with some of the folk from the funeral to help me understand more about my dad in his final years. Living so far away our communication was restricted to calls and even then few and far between.'

He offers a sympathetic, understanding smile. Maybe rehearsed? 'To be frank with you, Phil, I did not know your father very well. We met only once when he knew his time was almost up.'

'But the service?' My confused look speaking louder than my words.

'I know it sounds strange after the service and everything, but please believe I spoke with genuine love and respect for him as I would do any man from the parish. I think most who attended last week were coming from the same place, recognising his tenure here in the community. From what I gather, he was a very private person.'

I manage a half-smile.

'Maybe Reg can add some colour, he chose the hymns and spoke fondly of him to me before the service.'

I feel relieved my dad was not alone, even if only in spirit, and that he had the support and respect of the village. 'Can you put me in touch with Reg?'

'I probably shouldn't share his number, but what I can share with you is that he volunteers at the children's home up at Teyford and will be there tomorrow until 5ish.'

I finish my tea and thank the vicar again for the service with a warm handshake. 'If there is anything I can do,' he offers, studying my mischievous smile.

'There is maybe one small thing you can help me with. Your office kindly arranged the flowers via a family firm from Bournemouth, are there no local florists anymore?'

'Yes, of course, but just the usual high street chains. It was at the request of your father. He wanted a more personal touch, and to ensure we started on time, and of course for you to speak, they were his only asks.'

I feel good, too good to go home and sit in the empty house surrounded by to-do lists. I drive into the village, passing the fast-food chains and find a table at the Foxboro for some lunch. I am so pleased to see the Foxboro still going strong in a place full of changing demographics and identity. The Foxboro is like taking a step back in time.

The food is basic with tea served in mugs, each one from the owner's private collection. The menu is sketched on a blackboard behind the counter, although unlikely to have changed in a decade. In keeping with my surroundings, I order a corned beef and pickle sandwich on white, no seven different varieties of bread here to choose from here. Sitting at my table, I take in my surroundings. No mobile phones here, the odd person reading the Daily Mirror, an older lady engrossed in a book but mostly just folk sitting, looking out of the window, watching the world go by. I imagine it is always like this in the Foxboro, sometimes folk sit and think, sometimes they just sit. It is like time has stood still here, a tiny corner of Baysworth left untouched by the wave of commercialisation.

I pick up the local paper, the Dorset Herald, stained by what looks like an egg yolk and toast crumbs from this morning's serving. It makes some grim reading for this once-sleepy County; an OAP found dead in his flat, a young girl sexually assaulted on a night out, reports of drug dealing at local schools and a suspected paedophile ring busted in police raids. I read how the police broke up the alleged paedophile ring after searching a beach hut in Weymouth where the atrocities are believed to have taken place. The article includes a picture of the beach hut; a small wooden hut, tiny in size and a dirty mustard colour with a rusty lock. Residents were shocked that such atrocities could have taken place so close to the main beach where thousands visit in the summer, with one quoted as saying, '*You never know what goes on behind a closed-door even if it is right on your doorstep.*' The size and appearance of the beach hut is the mirror image of Donald's. I swallow hard, the air in café thickening, my breathing becoming heavier. My mind venture's into dark places once again.

Donald is front and centre in my thoughts. If he did shut the story down to protect others, it would have been above and beyond the call of duty, a debt much more significant than what I have been reading about from various whistleblower accounts. Would he risk a prison sentence for a handshake? Maybe the size of the prize was his freedom? My dad was always suspicious of him, and the time Jimmy spent with him. They must have had a severe falling out for them not to speak and for the police to warn my dad away from him. Maybe my dad suspected something, perhaps even made an accusation? But I know my dad, he would not have stopped there.

I drive home, still calculating my thoughts. I speed up to overtake the bin lorry just before it pulls into Hatch End, nothing worse than being stuck behind a bin lorry on a narrow road. As I pull into the empty drive, I have to veer left onto the grass just to avoid Donald's bin sitting proudly in the middle of the driveway. I get out of the car, hearing the lorry growing closer. Without thinking I grab the handle of his bin and wheel it to the back of my house, hidden from the sight of the approaching bin lorry. I feel like a naughty child playing hide and seek as I watch the refuge collector grabbing mine and loading it onto the raised platform to be emptied. As the truck pulls away, I wheel his back to the middle of the driveway, unable to hold back a smirk of satisfaction.

I sit down with a cup of tea already stressing about the bin, my conscious torn. I could swap the number stickers and give Donald my empty bin and take his full one. But two weeks is a long time though to wait for it to be collected again and I have clearing out to do. The doorbell halts my thoughts; the consequence of guilt catapulting me up in the air in fright. It is also an unfamiliar sound. I have been here for over a week, and it is the first visitor.

'Philip did your bin gets emptied today?' Donald asks, skipping the hello part.

'Urm, yes, I think so,' I am taken aback by his directness.

'Well did it or didn't it? I see it is round the back of your house, so did you wheel it back full or empty?' he stands staring into my eyes, hands on hips. 'It felt empty, but then there was not much in it in the first place,' I say with growing confidence, refusing to be intimidated.

'Damn those incompetent council bin men. You don't tip them at Christmas, and they think they have the right to mess you around, I'm phoning the council.' He shakes his head, his verdict delivered through his innate authority.

I think of some poor girl on the receiving end of his rant. 'Donald yours may have been left because it is so full, I read in the paper how they have gone Health & Safety mad and cannot lift anything heavier than 20kg. I remember them having a good look at it and maybe leaving a note on it, but it must have blown away, I would have run out for you to sort it, but I was on the phone.'

He shook his head with the fury of a victim and trudged back to his house, mumbling something about incompetence. He grinds to a halt and turns to me once again, adopting my

Columbo style I smirk to myself. He lifts his head high as if about to make an announcement. 'Actually, I called to ask for a favour. The damn airline company misplaced my suitcase from my recent trip and are due to deliver it back tomorrow morning, but I have an important appointment. They will not leave it without a signature, will you be in to receive it for me?'

My mind goes straight to the term appointment, so formal. I cannot help wondering what it may be. 'Err yes, of course, I am in tomorrow,' I finally reply having appeared to think about this far too much.

A simple nod and he turns again walking back to his house, the now familiar slam of his door closing down our conversation.

I set about cleaning the kitchen, scrubbing each stain on the surface and floor. I have lost track of time but notice the light fading outside and realising I have not had a drink. I feel a small sense of achievement and suddenly want to tell the world. I do the next best thing and call Caroline, who will be settling down to her Netflix. She answers sheepishly, the apprehension in her voice fuelled by the uncertainty on which Phil is calling no doubt. I apologise for the last time we spoke, admitting I was out of order, although privately I still have no recollection of what I said.

'I understand Phil, it would have been a tough day for you, and I am sorry you had to go through it alone, but the reason you are alone is not my fault, you cannot keep blaming me for everything.' The voice in my head argues back that I did not mention blame.

I tell her about what I found in my dad's private papers, and about my suspicions around Donald, and how I want to find the truth. I brace myself for her lecture on getting my life together,

54

to get back to work, to stop wasting my time and to move on.

'I think it is good for you, to re-visit the past, to ask questions, to find some closure. You have kept hold of the unknown for too long, without you realising it Phil, it defines you.'

I take a deep breath, I want to argue back, tell her she has no idea what defines me and what I think, but she reads my mind. 'You never open up, let anybody inside. It is like we all have to accept you as mysterious, but it does not offer anybody who loves or cares about you any comfort when this affection is unrequited. It was draining for me Phil, you never once made me feel secure.'

In all our arguments, I have never heard Caroline sound so measured with her thoughts, and it is like she is quoting somebody else. My recollection of our disagreements still feels raw. They would often degenerate into personal attacks, which escalated like a snowball each time, each of us knowing what buttons to press.

I know I won't sleep so I look for a distraction around the house, settling down in the kitchen to watch a squirrel outside the window. It darts around the garden searching for food. I admire its tenacity, and at the same time astonished by the destruction of the grass and plants it has left in its trail. If this were my house, my garden, I would be pissed off.

I open the door and feel the night chill biting at my face. I lift the cover from the old storage chest at the back of the house and pull out a bag of bird feed. I rip it open and walk the length of the garden pouring it over the fence onto Donald's side, knowing his flowerbed lies directly below. I stand in the kitchen and look out satisfied, and the squirrels have abandoned my dad's baron garden for rich pickings elsewhere. I open a bottle of wine; sleep will come after.

Chapter Fourteen – 8 days after

The doorbell chimes for the second time in two days. I sign my name on a small notepad as best I can, gripping the heavy suitcase in my other hand, causing me to drift off balance and writing at best a squiggle. I sit and stare at the carry-on size brown case. A leather badge showing off the designer brand on the front with far too many gold zips offering access to different compartments. I heard Donald's car leave only half an hour earlier, so I know I have the time if I have the inclination. I decided at 4.07 this morning that I would open the case and search it. I concluded there is already a trail of suspects should he discover someone has rifled through it, baggage handlers, security staff, lost property and most recently a delivery company, I would be bottom of his list of suspects.

I place the case on the dining room table and pull the biggest of the gold zips three-quarters of the circumference of the case, clothes springing out like a shaken beer overflowing. My immediate concern is being able to fit it back in. I lift out a couple of polo shirts, one dark blue and one a shade lighter with a small motif on the arm of two swords crossing. A pair of cargo shorts with a belt providing an imbalance to the rectangular shape it is folded to, a white linen shirt stained yellow on the cuffs, a pair of sandals and some white socks screwed in a perfect ball shape with some briefs. I pick each item out of the case and place carefully on the table like a police detective going through evidence. I am careful to put them on the table as I found them so I can return the items in roughly the same form. I pull out some cheap-looking wooden carvings of animals, a packet of tissues and see a folded tourist map of Bucharest. I pull out a hotel invoice stating *Europa hotel*, stating a double room for '*Mr Almoner*', a 3-night stay with some minibar items and three different taxes before the invoice amount. I worry I have the wrong suitcase and look to the door expecting the delivery man to be standing there realising his mistake.

I Google the hotel and find a rather basic looking three-star hotel in Ferentari, Bucharest. The hotel description prides itself on a quiet stay in a local neighbourhood and off the beaten track and tourist trail, yet close to the city. Tucked into the side of the case is a receipt for *Bellway Airport Transport* with details of a booking for Mr Donald Lloyd, 5 Hatch End, Baysworth. I smug to myself, so Donald is using a fake name.

I squeeze a blue pouch-like bag as a child does with a wrapped present; it has an Italian name on a gold crest. I reach inside to find a well-worn travel toothbrush, a small bottle of mouthwash, a sample size bottle of cologne, a comb, indigestion tablets, earplugs, and an eye mask. I empty the bag but still feel a bulky object to one side, and I find a discreet side pocket to the pouch accessed via a different zip. I pull out a small bottle of oil sticky on the outside with only about a third of the golden colour liquid remaining and a small dampened label half scratched away with foreign writing. I put my fingers in deeper, grabbing a small brown glass bottle with a sturdy black lid. I turn it in my palm to reveal a small label saying,

'*Amyl Nitrite*'.

Again, I jump on my laptop for insight and Google the term, opening the first article which describes it as, 'the most common type of poppers inhalant that is widely used as a recreational drug especially on the gay scene.' I smile and curse at the same time, 'got him,' I shout.

I read on, hungry for more revelations, I learn it was popular in the 1960s, giving an instant high as fumes are inhaled directly from the bottle. There is even an image of the same bottle that I have in my hand. It is considered a sex enhancer for gay men by relaxing the anal muscles. I connect this with why Donald booked into a discreet hotel under a pseudonym.

I go to the kitchen to make a coffee, and as I stand over the kettle boiling I think of the posh coffee and tea service in hotel rooms with complimentary biscuits, and I wonder why the Europa hotel? He is a wealthy man by all accounts, and I am sure Bucharest has plenty of reasonably priced five-star international hotels in the cultural quarter, old town or city centre. I return to my laptop and type in his location, 'Ferentari'. I read about its high crime rate, about its prostitution, and the number of what they describe as 'street children' that litter the streets, fuelling child abductions and child prostitution. I slam the laptop shut. I have him.

That sick bastard, I have got him.

My mind wanders to dark places as I sit at the table numbed by my finding. The initial adrenalin of finding evidence wearing off, the reality of his true persona takes over. A sickness returns to my stomach. My nausea transforms into a pure rage at the image of Jimmy, my clenched fists pure white in front of me. This has been going on for decades, and the man is over seventy years old. I cannot imagine how many victims there are.

I open a can of beer and drink it hungrily, three big gulps at a time, the bitter taste sitting nicely in my mouth. I look down at the table of Donald's possessions. I pack them away carefully when all I want to do is rip them up, throw them against the wall, to spit on them. I sit the case down by the front door, wondering back to his absence and what his appointment might be about. I open another can of beer.

I need a walk to clear my head and stop outside of Roger's house, how I wish he were here to make sense of all this. I write a note to give me a call when he is back. As I post it through his letterbox, I sense eyes on me and then a high-pitched voice addressing me.

'Who are you and what are you doing?'

I turn to see Roger's immediate neighbour. 'Hellloooo,' I sarcastically reply fuelled the beers. 'I am an old family friend and was posting a note to Roger.'

She looks at me fiercely, like she has chewed a wasp. Her face is thin, blonde hair so tightly pulled back it appears stuck on, dressed in lycra bottoms and a skin-tight top. She has a tight grip on her dog's collar, which has no interest in going anywhere. It is clear she feels threatened, although I don't know why, so I try and diffuse her hostility. 'I live, well my dad lives, I meant lived, at number 6.' No reaction.

'I am just visiting to sort the funeral and stuff, and as I say, I am an old friend of Roger.'

She looks me up and down again. 'He's not home.'

I see my opportunity. 'I know he is on holiday; do you know when he will be back.'

She looks put out that I asked her a question and her bellicose nature again takes over. 'If you were such good family friends you would know, wouldn't you?'

59

I genuinely have no response. I could have shared the whole emotional upheaval with my dad, but she showed no sympathy when I mentioned him. I could have told her of my strong suspicion that she shared the street with a paedophile and to channel her aggression elsewhere, but I suspect the very mention of the word would have her phoning the police on me. She seems Donald's type, although new money rather than old. I walk away and make a point of going back to the house as if to prove my identity, pathetic.

The first thing I see as I open my door is the suitcase staring back at me, and I boot it across the floor feeling an immediate sharp pain to my metatarsal, an old football injury flaring up.

I go to the fridge for a beer and take it to the back garden taking in the lengthening shadows from the woods behind the house. It is no surprise, my dad, no longer socialised if that is the new breed of neighbour. What could have happened to her in life that has turned her so bitter?

I think of Caroline and wonder about her response. She always said I was the aggressor, not in a violent way, least not intentionally but I was still suspicious and assumed the worst in people. Much like that woman. A scruffy man walks toward me. I immediately stand tall, give a stare. I was always hyper-vigilant to what constitutes a threat. I would feel angry when my own rules were broken, and sometimes my standards were a little warped. For many it is natural to mirror the persona you are faced with, so the innocent man walking towards me minding his own business feels threatened and replicates, resulting in a stand-off, sometimes an angry exchange of words, sometimes physical.

She always thought I was the aggressor because of my insecurities. Caroline would preach that, 'anger was a self-fulfilling prophecy, if you think, expect and look for the worst in people, they will often live up to your expectations. The subconscious, deletes the information that does not meet your expectations but inflates those that do, it is a blinkered view.' She would smile and then take my hands in hers and quote me her mantra 'the mind is a wonderful servant, but a lousy master.'

If I was labelled the angry man then Caroline was the opposite, all sunshine and rainbows, glass half full, Miss Positivity. I teased her, saying she just walked around handing out skittles, and to this day I don't know why I teased her unique nature, maybe because I knew I could never compete. It was never a competition, but she won.

'If I smiled at the same scruffy looking gentleman, he might just smile back.' She would preach.

My response was nothing if not predictable. I'd remind her that she was a pretty woman, and what man wouldn't smile back, maybe even wink.

She stuck with it. 'The voice in your head does not have to be an angry, threatening voice giving you orders, it can be soft, it can be gentle, it can speak to you very calmly and very slowly.'

I sniggered back, why not just tell me to count to ten. Anger is the subconscious bubbling up like with Donald now. I am fully aware of it, I know anger breeds anger, but I don't know how to stop it, I don't know if I want to stop it. I miss Caroline, that ray of sunshine. Towards the end of our relationship I mistook her happiness for our happiness.

Sitting amongst the stillness of the garden, I am haunted by a creeping sense of unease. I think back to my day. I forgot about visiting Reg, I got side-tracked entirely by Donald and finding the Amyl Nitrite in his suitcase, and with this flashback, the frustration immediately returns, stirring me into action.

I take a bottle of wine upstairs and sit on my bed, with my laptop poised. I find Donald's telephone number on 192.com, and without hesitation, phone it from my mobile, withholding my number. I hear the faint ringing sound through the wall, and I hear his footsteps, I imagine him waking up confused, worried, reaching for his slippers. I listen to him trudging down the stairs, his pace increasing, my attention goes to my phone as he picks up reciting his whole number back to me like my parents used to. I can hear the distress in his voice, I had given little thought to any plan, and so I just hang up.

I want him to be exposed for what he does, for what he did. I want him to worry about people knowing before the full exposure. I want him to sweat and squirm in anticipation. It is the worry and the lack of any control that will cause him the most pain, I have been there. My heart beats fast with excitement.

I navigate the web signing him up to numerous mailing lists, free trials, catalogues, scheduling sales calls and arranging a house valuation. Every search takes me down a new rabbit hole, new avenues of opportunities. I order him a taxi for the morning and sign him up to volunteering activities, all by using his full name, telephone number and address. The clock on the bottom left of my screen flicks to AM. I close the laptop satisfied I have done something today. I drift off to sleep, smugly satisfied at the upcoming barrage of annoyances to his life. Tomorrow is another day, more of the same.

Chapter Fifteen – 9 days after

I wake to a commotion, crashing sounds of metal and drilling. I sit up, forcing my eyes open to scan the room, expecting to see shadows. The bright sun fighting against the curtain puts me at ease instantly. I sit still, listening intently. I can hear raised voices coming from beyond the window. I think back to my actions last night with regret. This is my doing, I have caused this, and now I will have to watch the chaos unfold. I try picturing the scene of a taxi driver and Donald arguing, but the sounds throw me, it doesn't correlate. It is not one voice I hear, but many.

I pull back the curtain and to my horror see three young guys dressed in scruffy clothes strutting around outside Donald's house. One barks out orders above the radio noise, another has a cigarette in his mouth while carrying a huge metal pole above his head, the third is drilling bolts to hold them together. I watch them erecting the scaffolding against Donald's house. His car is not on the driveway, in its usual place is a rusty old truck with a further hundred metal poles piled high. I go downstairs and put the kettle on as is my routine. The noise volume increasing from outside, filtering into my kitchen. I slam my fridge shut, and I bang the coffee down against the worktop as if a justified response, wanting to be noticed. I stand over the boiling kettle, my inquisitive nature getting the best of me, I peer out of the window but see little at ground level and so return upstairs.

I try and calculate how much scaffolding is going up. Already it is up to half the height of the house. I try to distract myself but find myself returning to the window every couple of minutes. I see the taxi I ordered last night pull up, the taxi I thought would wake Donald up, would cause him stress, and maybe even an argument outside in his dressing gown. I did not envisage it being greeted and waved away by a six-foot tattooed labourer with a wrench in one hand and a cigarette in the other.

I step into the shower. The fierce water pressure is demanding the full attention of all my senses and a quick release.

On turning the tap off the outside noise invades my conscience once again. I wrap a towel around me and take my position at the window. The scaffolding continues to grow beyond the second floor and onto the adjoining roof. Each time a new pole is connected, a sheet of plastic is discarded towards the ground. I watch with frustration as the rubbish gets picked up by the wind some landing in my garden. I could go out and complain, but I will wait for my real target to return home, a perfectly reasonable excuse to confront him.

I need to get out of the house, away from the noise. I reverse out of my drive, not even glancing in the direction of the scaffolding or reprobates strutting about like they own the place. Still no sign of Donald's car, he scheduled this disruption so of course would have made plans for the day. *Bastard.*

I drive over to Teyford, a small town boasting a couple of retail parks and the children's home where I hope to catch Reg or Anna. I appreciate the fifteen-minute drive to cool off a bit, although the annoyance stays with me. I do not know if either is there, but it is less embarrassing than admitting to the vicar I forgot and wanting to know their shift patterns for the week, like some kind of stalker.

The children's home sits isolated at the end of a single track on the outskirts of Teyford, enclosed by tall pine trees that darken the windows. The stone driveway makes an excessive crunching noise as I reverse into the visitor space. A couple of ageing concrete steps delivers me to an imposing wooden door painted racing green to brighten up the 1950s redbrick building. Its compartmentalised shape, surrounding land and location makes me think this would have been originally a school. A large wooden sign says 'Camwell Lodge, C of E,' other than that there is no reference to its purpose or use. I slam the old brass knocker hard on the sodden wood door that feels 10cm thick. Even the brass letterbox is exaggerated in size and stiff to disturb. To my left is a big bay window, glass as thick as a beer bottle. I hold up my palms against it to deflect the glare and see a lady standing almost to attention in front of me. She does that thing of mouthing something to me, although I have no idea what, regardless, I return a smile.

'Hello, do come in, how can I be of assistance?' Marjorie says all in one go opening the front door.

She is the lady from the window, dressed in a bright green woolly cardigan with her name badge sitting proudly, and small round glasses sitting on the end of her nose. The inside of the house is a mash-up of old and new. A grand wooden twisted staircase dressed in a horrible cheap rubber matt running up the centre to control the noise I presume. Lined up against the back wall are sofas and armchairs of contrasting colour, shape and size, reminiscent of a second-hand furniture shop. The overflow of plastic chairs stacked up under the stairs and numerous posters depicting the many rules next to a first aid box fixed to the wall.

'I was hoping Reg or Anna might be in today. I am a family friend of theirs.' I proudly proclaim.

'Oh no I am sorry,' Marjorie relies with concern, holding her hands in front of her. 'Anna no longer visits us because of her arthritis, but Reg does, although only once a week so he can be at home more to care for poor Anna. His day was yesterday. I am sorry you had a wasted journey, maybe you could visit next week?'

No, not next week. I now need Marjorie's help. 'I am John Jenkins' son, Phil. I met Reg and Anna at the funeral last week.'

Marjorie took a step towards me and reached for my hand, holding it in her cold, bony fingers, 'I am so sorry for your loss, John was a good man, a welcome visitor here, and he will be sorely missed.'

I was taken aback. In my pursuit of Reg and Anna, I completely forgot what sparked my interest; it was they who informed me that my dad volunteered here occasionally. *But what did he do here?*

Marjorie stares at me, as if reading my mind, or more likely the confused look on my face. 'Anything I can help you with Phil?'

'Maybe. Dad and I,' I began and paused, feeling sheepish. 'We didn't communicate often.' Finding the words proved more difficult than I'd expected in front of Marjorie with her permanent smile and look of sympathy etched across her face. 'Can you tell me what he did here exactly?'

She pauses and takes out from her cardigan pocket a crumpled tissue to dab her nose. 'Mr Jenkins led some classes here for the children and held some one-to-one sessions with some of our more challenging children, like a mentor.'

I feel my face screwing up in confusion, prompting Marjorie to continue. 'Marie would know more as she runs the outreach program coordinating with all of our volunteers. She is teaching a class at the moment. Maybe I could ask her to call you?'

I run my hand through my hair, pulling at it and keep my eyes to the ground out of sight from Marjorie, not wanting to show her my frustration. I write my number on a post-it with my name and my dad's name. I stand in the hallway staring at the children's paintings proudly displayed on the wall, wondering what exact wisdom or life experience my dad could have passed on to these lost children.

As I get in my car to drive home, I remember the chaos that awaits. I decide to take a detour for an early lunch. I order a pint while waiting for the kitchen to open then order sausages and mash and another pint. *Why was my dad visiting the children's home?* I drag myself out of my trance and look around me to see I am still the only customer as I drop off my empty plate at the bar and head home.

I pull up to an empty driveway, no sign of either the scaffolders or Donald, but my eyes are drawn to a parcel left outside his front door. Without much thought, I walk over and pick it up to take a look. Hungry for more evidence, and without thinking too hard, I tuck it under my arm and carry it inside my dad's house. I google the company name it has been dispatched from, to reveal a pharma company specialising in online medication. I hold the parcel in front of me feeling a sudden unease, a shadow? I turn and freeze at the sight of Donald standing in my hallway, eyes fixed on me holding his parcel.

'Sorry, didn't mean to startle you, the door was open. Thank you for taking in my parcel.'

67

Behind his left shoulder, I watch a plastic sheet getting picked up by the wind and being whisked off the scaffolding attached to his house.

'I did request they just leave at my front door, but you know these delivery folk, not the sharpest.'

Scattered all over the driveway are abandoned tools and materials, heavy-duty bags stuffed full, planks of wood and of course the offending radio.

'They would rather bang on the door of a neighbour, terribly sorry for the inconvenience.'

Every patch of his house is shielded behind scaffolding, ready to knock down and re-build?

I tune back into Donald only to see him walking away from me, the parcel having been removed from my hands and he is carrying his suitcase. That's it? No mention of the monstrosity that is evolving right in front of us?

'Donald, hold on a minute,' I demand. 'What is all this with the scaffolding? What is going on?'

I can see as he stands straighter, clears his throat and points his eyes to the sky that he has rehearsed his response. 'Some renovations, nothing too major, I have the necessary planning permission.' He turns to walk away again, but I follow him this time.

'But you can't, I am about to put the house on the market, you know this, how long will it take?'

He shrugs his shoulders. 'I can, as I say, I have the necessary permission. It won't take long.' I stand dumbfounded. The nerve of the man, not even having the decency to discuss with me beforehand and hiding behind planning permission as his approval, his right, and nothing else matters. I shake my head towards his front door, already slammed shut.

I throw my dad's clothes into two piles, my mind elsewhere. How can he be so arrogant? And just walking away from me like that. Bloody Donald. Two piles, charity or disposal. I find a strange assortment of sports tops, waterproof trousers, hiking boots. I admit to myself I did not know this man at all as I hold up a bright pink shirt with flowers on the cuffs.

Hearing movement again from next door I leap to the window and watch Donald load his car with the same suitcase he took from me earlier and place a jacket carefully on the passenger seat before driving away. Of course, he is going away to escape the impending noise, the disruption, the disturbance. I accept this as an invitation to walk around the back of his house to see for myself what is going on.

Much like the front, it is covered in scaffolding with wooden planks running the perimeter of the first level and planks of wood to form a makeshift platform. The garden is a mess, strewn with plastic covers blowing around, bits of wood cutting lying on the grass abandoned, nails scattered, empty boxes and even crisp packets and coke cans from their 10 am lunches. The scaffolding is firmly entrenched into his flower bed standing toe to toe with the fence.

I return to the front of his house and open his recycling bin, lifting out the box stuffed of paper and card. Underneath, where mine is full of bottles and cans, sits a solitary empty can of beans. I carry the heavy-duty plastic box into my kitchen and start leafing through his recycled papers, desperate to build a better profile of this man.

A couple of shopping catalogues, some utility bills, and a quotation from a building company for a house extension. I pull it out and study it line by line. The quote is for a ground floor extension, two bedrooms and en-suite with the required scaffolding. *Renovation?* He is doubling the size of his house. I screw it up tight and throw it hard against the kitchen wall. How can he possibly be planning such a massive building project at his age and how on earth did he get planning permission? I grab hold of the box wanting to smash it to pieces, but something catches my eye. I pull out his mobile phone and broadband bill listing his private email address and mobile number. I carefully fold it and place in my pocket, returning the box to his recycle bin, my confidence rising.

I need to up the ante. My activity last night would only inconvenience him, *what if he didn't even notice?* I need to be less subtle and start testing his resolve. I have his personal details now. Masquerading as Donald Lloyd, I start registering his details on gay websites, inviting a response, inviting awkward liaisons. I lose myself in this unfamiliar world as I uncomfortably write about fetishes, and upload fake profile pictures. I find local blogs and gay chat groups which I register and add his details, opening the floodgates. A little calmer I grab a can of beer and settle back on the couch, more confident I can hurt him. I want to hurt him.

I want to uncover his mask.

Chapter Sixteen – 10 days after

The phone ringing. I lay in bed listening to it embedded into my dream before I realise it is real. I stand, head pounding and answer groggily. I apologise to the solicitor for the delay and promise to get the financial paperwork over to him today. I look out my window taking a second or two to focus and adjust to the brightness. There is an old pale blue van in his driveway marked 'Marsden Builders,' the front dashboard looking like a bin has been emptied onto it with newspapers, coke cans, cigarette packets squashed between the dashboard and front window. A Portsmouth FC air freshener hangs from the mirror. I hate Portsmouth.

I watch as a middle-aged guy walks up Donald's driveway. He has receding hair, three-day stubble, and a heavily stained jumper that sits above his exposed belly. He is holding up his stained trousers, phone held to his ear in his other hand. I watch him ducking and diving outside the front door looking for something. He tilts a plant pot and tucking his phone to his ear, he reaches down to pick up a key. He slots it in the door and pushes it wide open, walking in without hesitation. Despite the cold weather he wedges the door open and in follows a couple of much younger lads from the van, in similar attire, but very much apprentices. I stand rooted to my window watching them carry toolboxes and make return trips to empty the contents of the van in the house.

I force myself to get dressed and grab my car keys, needing to extract myself from the horror show unveiling from my window.

I have a horrible sense of déjà vu in the supermarket. The pitiful looks from the suits buying breakfast on the go, the horror from mothers protecting their small children and giggles from schoolkids stocking up on crisps and chocolate. All eyes are on me and my basket of food necessities with enough beer and wine for weeks already knowing I will make a return trip in a couple of days.

When Caroline and I were together, the grocery shopping was my task, although I didn't find it a chore. I took pleasure in surprising her with simple offerings. It could be as simple as a cupcake or her favourite chocolate bar, the gesture being she was in my thoughts as I followed the herd of broken trolleys and screaming kids around the aisles. I always tried to be creative, seeking out new dishes for us to try, making a new desert or trying an exotic fruit. Shopping is easier for one, but more fun for two.

As I turn the final corner in Hatch End, I hit the brakes taking in the sight before me. I am greeted by what looks like a wrecker's yard. I count three vans, an old Volkswagen Polo, and sitting in the centre of the driveway is a big yellow skip. I weave between cars and vans having to manoeuvre past the skip by putting my left tyres onto the grass. My dad would have hated this. He would have been out here, fist-waving and shouting at them all. But look how that approach worked out? Cautions from the police.

I open my car door to a wall of noise with drilling, banging and shouting all competing with music blaring from the sizeable paint-stained stereo sitting pride of place on top of the skip. Nobody turns a head as I carry my shopping into the house, I am invisible to their world.

The noise of the builders commands my attention, and I am continually drawn to the window to watch, unable to feel at ease in the house. I grab a four-pack of beers which have barely had time to cool in the fridge and hop over the sty to the woods. My feet are squelching with each step, mud covering my inadequate white trainers, weighted down with each step, eyes on the mud to avoid the puddles. I walk until it is quiet, no music, no drilling, and no shouting, taking a seat on a fallen tree which feels damp against my jeans. I reach into the plastic carrier bag tugging a can free from the plastic and pulling back the ring pull, generating the familiar fizzing of beer covering the top of the can with a layer of froth. The beer is warm, heightening the aggressive taste of the alcohol, I drink it fast. I see no-one, I hear nothing, and I slip away into a dreamy trance.

My attention is drawn to voices, and the crunching of leaves nearing me. I pull myself up from the tree, the back of my legs stiff and cold. I shuffle my feet amongst the brown leaves and empty beer cans feeling the blood returning. I see the little boy before he sees me, bright yellow boots up his legs with a padded coat zipped above his chin, the sleeves rolled up to free his little fingers. He runs towards me using all of his body, a mop of yellow hair flirting over his brown eyes. Our eyes meet, and he holds up a small stick without breaking stride, I crouch down to his level, his smile widening with pride.

'Thomas stop.' The boy freezes upon the instruction from behind him, his dad shuffling into view through the branches.

73

Slender in build, his formal hairstyle and trendy glasses out of place amongst his weekend wet gear, more suited to the midweek suit. He looks straight past the boy and focuses in on me.

'Thomas leave that man alone, come back to daddy now,' holding out his arms not daring to come any closer. The boy holds out his stick as far as he can reach, 'Stick Man,' he shouts and then swivels to face his nervous-looking dad. I watch them walk away, but I don't see the dad holding the little hand poking out of the yellow jacket, I see myself lifting the boy onto my shoulders, Caroline by our side with a beaming smile for her boys. I stay crouched watching our family trundle away, and take my final swig from the can.

The look on that dad's face is imprinted on my mind as I trudge back to the house, the initial buzz of alcohol turning quickly to self-loathing. His stare was one of alarm and fright as his eyes met mine, igniting his protective instinct to protect son as he approached me. Me, a middle-aged man standing alone in a forest gripping hold of my last can of beer, and not even midday. My sweater stained in beer, trampling on empties, bloodshot eyes and the edge. That little boy will grow up realising there is no greater need in childhood as strong as the need for your father's protection.

I think to my own dad. I think back to when we took a boat out in Brixham during a holiday. We had been searching for the legendary Bluefin tuna, a rare sighting off the coast of Devon. At 12-years-old, Jimmy was far more confident and agile on the boat than I and competitive. Who could spot the tuna first? Dad pulled me in close as he spotted the shimmering white torpedo-shaped body splashing in front of us. We celebrated our find, and our win and called Jimmy across without response.

74

My dad shouted louder before the boat rocked, allowing us to catch sight of Jimmy in the sea, arms aloft, and terror strewed across his face as he disappeared under. My dad stood and jumped in as one, crashing hard into the sea, arms thrashing frantically before wrapping them around Jimmy and pulling him up to the surface. He lifted him back on the boat and hovered over his flat, lifeless body, blue veins flashing beneath his translucent skin. Holding Jimmy's nose between his thumb and forefinger, he gave mouth to mouth, calmly counting out loud as he pushed against his young chest. First, a cough, then a second cough followed by the release of water from his mouth, his eyes opened, and his forming smile brought the colour back to his cheeks. My dad sat him upright and hugged Jimmy tightly, he hugged us both tightly, tears running down his cheeks. *'I love you boys, my boys,'* he said.

It is the perfect memory of my dad, and as he did with us for hours on that boat, I cling to it when I need to, my dad, the hero. He may not have spent an hour reading bedtime stories or making us breakfast, but I know he would have done anything to protect us. Of course, he had to spot the danger first, even if it was only next door.

I kick off my muddy trainers at the front door and run straight to the bathroom for a pee, leaving a trail of damp footprints from my wet socks. The noise next door has subsided, and I look at my watch to see it is only midday, must be on a lunch break. I stack together my dad's financial statements and place them in an oversized envelope for the solicitor. The building site continues to aggravate me. I want to go out there, all guns blazing, demanding the noise to stop, and demanding neighbourhood respect takes precedence over self-indulgence. *I need to stay in control.* I have to conform to our bureaucratic state and go through the appropriate channels. Only a faceless administration will hear my disgust, identifying me by reference number. I search online for the local authority building controls website to see for myself the planning permission. Entering his postcode and house number I find an application marked '*approved*' for new double glazed windows and painting of façade, submitted only a month ago, the taste of bitterness sours my mouth.

My fist clenches as I consider his arrogance, his sense of entitlement, his condescending nature assuming nobody dare challenge him. I search the site further for details on the complaint's procedure. I hammer at the keyboard, completing the required form of the noise complaint, each box a soapbox for my disgust, typed in capital letters and peppered with exclamation marks. I google a few legislative acts and gleefully quote them in my report of Donald's violation against the original planning application.

I open a beer toasting my progress and imagine the suits and clipboards arriving at Donald's house tutting at his non-compliance and disregard for the system. I notice a reply at the top of my inbox from the Planning department and smile with renewed faith at their efficiency. I hastily double click to open it and read a *thank you for my email which will be responded to within 72 hours.* I snap the laptop closed, just as the noise starts up again next door.

I settle on the sofa engrossed in cheesy Western films until daylight fades. I feel the need to shove food in my mouth, although not particularly hungry so I pierce a film lid and place another non-descript meal in the microwave, opening a bottle of red as if to formalise dinner time. The soft humming of the microwave gives way to silence, and I realise the builders must have finished for the day. I sit at the dining table in the living room, thinking of Donald. I can see how loathing can drive you insane. It is consuming, antagonising only myself. I am full of spite, yet I continue with it, the endorphins rising, needing a release.

I feel drunk, and with a beautiful, carefree feeling and misplaced confidence, I put on my shoes, still caked in drying mud, and walk over the drive to next door. I reach down to the plant pot and pick up the single silver Yale key from under it. I slot it in the keyhole, turn it slowly to the left and gently ease the door open with none of the brazenness of the builder this morning.

I step into Donald's house and stand in the living room as I did on 19th February 1986. So much looks the same, maybe a different carpet but the same colour, different wallpaper but the same style, and the same oak smell. The room is set up as I remember, an armchair in front of a TV, a wooden bookcase, the same desk perhaps and green leather office chair with same grandfather clock ticking, but so much louder. I have no plan, but I feel powerful, I feel in control walking around his house, uninvited, invading his privacy.

I sit down at his desk, his calendar staring back at me, three days marked with a B which I now know to be Bucharest. A small box for today's date and tomorrow both labelled with the letter E which is repeated on highlighted days next week, and every week after that. I open a long slim drawer that sits directly under his desktop. It is separated into small compartments which are filled with a box of matches, some coins, post-it notes, business cards, and letters. I flick through the letters; many are printed on headed papers with the words '*Baysworth Masonic Lodge*' across the top. I read a couple of boring monthly

77

newsletters about the finances of the lodge, about some travels of their brothers, about an upcoming gala. Nestled to the bottom of the draw is an expensive-looking oak frame, its contents missing.

I force myself to slow down and think. *Stay in control.* I stand rooted to the spot and take in my surroundings. Everything is so neat and tidy, everything has its place. *He must have OCD.* I afford myself a knowing smile, of course he does, explaining all those lectures given to us when we were kids trampling on his garden or kicking the ball into his flowers. We bore the consequences as kids, but now it provides me with the perfect platform for disruption. Perfect for causing confusion and frustration, more painful than merely stealing or wrecking the place, which can be blamed on the builders. I want to mess with his head, so I start moving things around, swapping some of his old paintings around, moving his lamp to the opposite side of his desk, placing the remote control in the fridge. I move quicker now, full of purpose. I want him to start questioning his sanity, and I want to keep him up at night just as Jimmy did, scared of his dreams. The cruellest attack is that of the mind, the perfect disorder for someone who needs order.

The persistent ticking of the grandfather clock competes with the battle planning in my head, deafening me to reason, logic, and conventional rules of being a sane person. Donald is a criminal on the loose. As I step slowly to the stairs, the room suddenly illuminates, I freeze, feeling exposed in the light and staring at my shadow on the wall. I hold my breath and close my eyes, waiting for a voice. I slowly blow the air from my cheeks. The only sound continues to be my exaggerated breaths competing against the tick of the clock. I slowly turn just as another light flicks on, and I wince again at the flash of light. There is nobody here, I breathe out in relief, and I slump down resting my heavy arms on my knees. The timer for the lights ensures the room is lit like a beacon.

I continue upstairs to his bedroom. As with downstairs, it is immaculate, nothing out of place. He has pills all over his bedside table. If I was smart, I could swap some of these around, formulating the perfect combination to cause maximum discomfort. That's what would happen in the movie, I could google it tonight.

I catch sight of myself in the mirror, I stare hard, confused in my thoughts. Is this me now? Someone who breaks into another man's house. If I read about this in the paper, I would be the first to judge. I would be disgusted. I would demand a prison sentence for such a personal violation of some poor old man's home, maybe he was a war veteran, what a total lack of respect.

Standing in front of the mirror, only half my face lit by the soft moonlight through the window, I think back to why I am here, for Jimmy, and for all those other victims. I see them locked in their rooms, I feel their misplaced shame, and I feel their loneliness, nobody protecting them, nobody fighting for them. I will fight for them. The face in the mirror smiles back.

I move some everyday items like his toothbrush and shampoo, place a t-shirt where his hand towel should be, taking out a lightbulb and swapping his sock drawer, and underwear draw around. I have altered enough in the house for him to be confused but not enough for him to be sure. I am also conscious that the house is lit up with curtains open, my shadows long, I would be easily visible if someone were to walk past. I replace the key under the plant pot and walk the hop, skip and jump distance to my front door. My adrenaline still high as I reach for a well-earned drink and settle back on the sofa.

My moment of contemplation is disturbed by a one-line text from Caroline, '*Have you put the house on the market?*' Apart from referencing it in protests to Donald about the impact of his building site, I had not given it a single thought until now. It will need more than cleaning the kitchen, and I do not have the time right now.

I lie in bed, tossing and turning, restless. I try and void my mind of thoughts but keep returning to Donald. His image, his house all too consuming. I look across to the wall, only hours ago I was standing just the other side of the partition, in his room. He was at my mercy and still is. Already I want to return.

Chapter Seventeen – 11 days after

For the second successive morning, I wake up to the phone ringing. I was only dozing, so I am much more responsive when Marie from the children's home wishes me a good morning and continues without waiting for a response. 'I am sorry I missed your visit yesterday. I understand your father passed away, and you would like to know a little more about what he did here at Camwell Lodge?' She sounds serious, almost suspicious. I explain how I had lost touch, and I was trying to understand more about him.

She continued in the same tone, 'I think we should meet in person so I can explain in some more detail, but not here at Camwell. How about 9.30 Wednesday morning in Costa Coffee, it's my day off, we can talk off the record as it were?'

It was clear Marie was not comfortable talking to me on the phone, maybe what she had to tell me was delicate, perhaps that's why she mentioned the term 'off the record.' There was no compassion or sympathy offered when mentioning my dad's passing. Frustratingly, I only think about this after I agree to meet her and have put the phone down.

I put the kettle on and take in the quietness, no weekend overtime for the builders next door thankfully. I think back to my actions at Donald's house. Despite being under the influence of alcohol and driven by vengeance, I have no regrets. It felt good. I playback when I thought he had caught me red-handed in his house, when the timer turned on the lights. If he had been standing behind me, what would I have done? I imagine going for him, striking him hard with my right fist, then with my left into his chest, watching him hit the floor in slow motion, one big boot into him. I feel my body tense up, teeth grinding, fist clenched as I imagine this. It feels good. Fight or flight, I stand and fight, for Jimmy, maybe I am 30 years late, but I was powerless then, without knowledge or life years. Now I am driven by revenge, for my family.

I hear a car outside and go to the window to see Donald taking his small case out of the boot. I watch as I have watched him all week, but this time I know where he has been and when he was due home, I feel a sense of power, even if all I know is the initial E for his whereabouts. He walks around his house like the Lord of the Manor inspecting the scaffolding. I watch him until he steps inside the house. I take pleasure for the second time as I imagine him staring at a painting on the wrong wall or searching for his remote control.

It's late Saturday morning, and I know Caroline will be just home from her spin class. I call her. I tell her more about Donald, about finding the poppers in his suitcase, about researching where he had been for his short break. She, predictably, sounds disappointed that I went through his personal belongings and warns me about jumping to conclusions. I claim my reasoning again but this time she stops me.

'Phil, I can hear the anger building in your voice, you will think it is justified, and I know you are focused on revenge, but my concern is for you, and I do not think this will end well,' she says in a non-patronising way. 'It has always been the same with you, needing someone to blame. This time it is Donald, before it was your boss, before that your mum, your dad before again. Can you not see, whoever angers you, controls you?'

She is right, she always is, although it usually takes me far longer to accept it. 'What would you do Caroline? I cannot let it go; doing nothing will cause me more pain.'

'I think Phil, you need more evidence, and you need to talk to Jimmy's friends, you need to find out from the police if Donald has any criminal history of this sort of thing, build a case and then let the authorities take over.' It's not what I wanted to hear, but I needed to hear it.

I pull out the school yearbook from my dad's box of papers and flick through until finding Jimmy's class photo. It has the names beneath the class, and I sit the photograph up against my laptop and begin searching Facebook. Some of the more familiar names like 'Oliver Davies' have thousands of matches, so I refine the search to Dorset. I play a detective trying to recognise a 14-year-old boy in a 45-year-old man whose picture is likely them standing on a rock, or holding a baby, or in a wedding suit. One of the names shows a profile picture taken probably not too long after the class picture, I recognise him straight away on the list of 'James Finley's'.

My eyes are also drawn to his full profile name listed as 'James Finley RIP.' I click on his profile and see confirmation of his hometown Baysworth, Dorset. I scroll down and view hundreds of condolences. The commonality between them is the message *'taken too soon'* with plenty of references to the prime of his life. *Taken? Like Jimmy was taken?* I google 'James Finley Dorset death,' but nothing materialises. The condolences appear from September 1989, a month after I relocated with mum to Chichester, and also a month after the story broke in the local newspaper of the sexual abuse investigation at the school.

I google again, referencing the school and his name. Nothing. I read through the condolences for the second time looking for any reference to the cause of his death. I read one that offers sympathies to his parents Fergal and Daphne Finley. There are four Finleys in the phone book and only one F.G Finley. I hurriedly phone the number, but no answer.

I send out 15 friend requests in total with a cut and paste concise note that I am Jimmy's brother and wanted to check a couple of things regarding his schooldays, giving no hint of the severity so as not to alarm. I am not a big Facebook user, too many fake lives being played out. While I am here though I check Caroline's page, she has recently changed her profile picture to an old one that I took of her on holiday in Tuscany. Her long hair is blowing slightly in the wind, and she has a royal blue tight t-shirt matching her eyes and a glass of white wine, boasting her trademark huge smile. My profile picture is of Caroline and me drunk in a bar in Manchester at her Uni reunion ten years ago, but I don't think any of my 11 friends on Facebook care or will notice if I change it now. Already today, I have spent more time social networking than I have in the past ten years.

I make myself a sandwich and a coffee for lunch, bypassing the shelf full of beer in the fridge, I need a clear head. For some reason I am nervous when I telephone the police, I do not want to give them my identity for risk of association. I want information, very personal information and I call the non-emergency number to ask how I could go about seeking confirmation of any convictions for an individual.

'Yes sir we can help, the process is straight forward'. The

operator has a perfect telephone voice, a comforting middle-class English accent straight from the Home Counties, no danger of anything being lost in translation.

'Two processes, depending on if you are a potential employer or public service official with good reason.' I hesitate, unable to justify either. The operator fills the pause, recognising I am in unchartered territory.

'You will, of course, need to complete a request form for either.' Mayday Mayday.

'And of course, provide the necessary evidence of being the employer or public service official.' I am sinking.

'The person of interest will also receive a notification. We ensure a transparent process.' Sunk.

'I just need to know what the Police have on somebody.' I plead, hearing the desperation in my voice.

'Another option available is the subject access request from the Data Protection Act 2018, giving you the right to ask if the police hold any personal data about you.' Her accent begins to irritate me, sounding monotone without emotion. Computer says no mentality.

'But that is based on my record only, I want to check up on my neighbour.' As I say this out loud, I know how ridiculous it sounds, and I hold my phone away from my ear poised to slam it down hard.

'Do you believe your neighbour possess a threat to a child sir?'

'Yes. More than just a threat, spending hours alone with him, grooming him.'

'Anyone who looks out for the welfare of a child can enquire. It is known as Sarah's law. To apply for a disclosure of the information, you will be interviewed face to face by a Police

Officer who will need to verify your information about the child in question, and we aim to respond within 45 days. You say your neighbour spends time alone with the child, was this recently?'

'About 30 years ago.' My voice slows and tails off as I put down the receiver.

I open a beer, justifying that my pursuit for the criminal check will be an online activity going forward, without the need to talk to anyone and certainly not face to face. My searches take me to an online form for the ACRO (criminal records office). I can request any police records against my name, except I don't use my name, I simply log in as Donald. I do not get very far when I am requested to send in a scanned copy of a driving license and proof of address, the other details I can fake, such as a signature. I will also need to check his date of birth. Thankfully, I know how and where to access this information. I just need Donald to leave the house.

I need a break from the screen and drive into the village. I buy my lottery ticket for tonight, always the same numbers combining the birthdays of Jimmy, myself, and Caroline. I pop into a new posh deli that has just opened in the high street; they still have balloons on the counter from their grand opening three days ago. I scan the shelves, astounded at the prices. I assumed local produce would be cheaper, fewer transport costs, as all we hear in the news is the rising cost of logistics. I treat myself with a homemade cottage pie to be warmed in the oven, not microwave, and a bottle of Chateauneuf du Pape. It is the weekend, after all.

I could have eaten at the best restaurant on the high street for the same price of my meal to be heated at home but eating out for one is not appealing. I sit in the deli and have a coffee, taking the chance to check my phone - you are never alone with a phone - no notifications on Facebook. I also look up Fergal Finley's number to try and contact him again. His address is listed and on my way home. I decide to call in, more personal I conclude.

Marlborough Court is old money. The private road boasts around 15 significant detached properties, each sitting in an elevated position from the road and most hiding behind big iron gates. Thankfully number seven does not, although I still choose to leave my car on the street and walk the 30 yards up to the door. The house is double fronted, huge bay windows with ivy growing up the façade. Two identical black BMWs sit on the drive. I ring the doorbell and take a step back to read the various warnings that door to door sellers are not welcomed, how I have entered a neighbourhood watch area and how I should smile as I am on camera right now. I suddenly become conscious of my appearance, I have made little effort with my attire, to shave or to even flatten my hair since the funeral, and the red warning light must be flashing as they observe me at their front door on camera.

Mr and Mrs Finley open the door wide, standing side by side, looking surprised to see somebody standing the other side even though I rang the bell.

'I am sorry to disturb you, my name is Phil Jenkins. I used to go to school with your son, and I have just returned to the area and only just found out about his passing.'

Mrs Finley looks to the ground, the mere mention of her son passing no doubt opening wounds that will never heal. Mr Finley looks at me closely as if trying to place my face or name.

'So you were you a pal of wee James?' he asks further qualifying my intrusion, spoken in a soft Edinburgh accent.

'We went to the same school, Bayswoth, I was a bit younger,

but he was good pals with my older brother, Jimmy Jenkins.'

'Jimmy Jenkins,' Mr Finley's eyes widened as he repeats the name, 'Poor Jimmy Jenkins, who took his own life while at the school?' he asks.

I break eye contact and clear my throat. 'Yes.' I say, unable to find more words. Fergal raises his eye-brows, without a trace that of awareness of his forthrightness, he leans into me trying prize more out of me. 'He was my brother, and the truth is, I am trying to find out more information about him, maybe even find out why he did what he did.' I still struggle with the word suicide.

With a pained expression and gasp, Mrs Finley taps him on the arm. She shoots him a lethal glare before turning to me tenderly. 'I am Daphne, and this is Fergal. You better come in for a cup of tea.'

Chapter Eighteen – 11 days after

Daphne sets down the tray of china cups, sugar bowl, milk jug, over-sized teapot, and shortbread biscuits. The room is adorned with framed photographs and portraits all depicting happier times of graduations, weddings, christening's and a 70th birthday party. I sit on the edge of the Great Chesterton sofa, besieged by cushions. Fergal and Daphne take an arm-chair each, the glass coffee table between us, the formalities complete it seems.

'A tragedy what happened to wee Jimmy, hit the school hard for many years after, cracking wee footballer too,' Fergal says, with a faraway look in his eyes as he reminisces. 'They still have a plaque up at the school, a memorial stone.'

'Oh, I didn't know that.' *Why didn't I know that?* Did mum and dad go to the unveiling of the plaque or was it after we left so just dad? I should feel pride that his life was recognised by the school my thoughts are cynical, imagining it as a peace offering.

'And what about James, is there also a plaque for him?' I ask.

'No, James had left Baysworth a couple years before, he was on a gap year when he passed,' Daphne answered.

Of course he was. I naively think of him as fourteen just like Jimmy, forgetting life moved on. I picture the newspaper headlines appearing just a month before his death. 'May I ask, how did James die?'

Fergal edged forward in his seat. 'A jet ski accident in Thailand, the silly wee boy was showing off and came off the thing hitting his head on some rocks.'

I could see him keeping the traditional stiff upper lip, but also see the emotion creeping into his eyes.

'I am sorry for your loss, I see even now it still is difficult.' I want to ask more about the school, about the allegations, but I see the emotion building.

We talk more about mundane topics like the traffic in Baysworth. As I stand to leave, Daphne offers me a window. 'You said that you were interested in knowing more about your wee Jimmy, what are you looking for exactly?' I know what to say but hesitate before sitting back down recognizing their fragile state.

Joining my hands together and bowing my head as if in prayer before I answer. 'Do you know if he was happy at school?' I lift my eyes to see them look at each other confused by my open question so personal.

'What I mean is.' I can't expect them to know Jimmy's state of mind, I don't even know if he and James were close. 'As I was clearing out the house Mrs Finley, I found an old newspaper article in my dad's possessions.' I glance at Daphne who sits motionless. 'It reported on sexual abuse investigations against the teachers of Baysworth Secondary, and it was around the time Jimmy took his own life.' I keep my head bowed this time imagining they are hearing this for the first time, imagining they meet each other's gaze.

I feel Fergal's hand on my shoulder before I hear his voice. 'There was some talk of Jimmy changing schools the year before, but the newspaper thing was just a crazy crank call, nothing to it.'

I stare up at Fergal, shocked by his instant dismissal, disappointed too, 'Its time I left, thank you for the tea, Mr and Mrs Finley,' I stand and let myself out, feeling lost in a world I do not know. I need to get home.

Through the door, I charge straight for my laptop and check my Facebook notifications, desperate for another try. I have one new friend, Victoria Dobson. Alongside the announcement of our new friendship is her profile picture, short blonde hair, a gold cross around her neck resting on a light blue poloneck jumper. Her picture is not in an exotic location, and neither is she hanging off a guy, just her looking straight into the camera, it could easily be a passport picture, a beautiful passport picture.

I click on her page and scroll through her Facebook life. It is very unassuming, much like my own. She was the author on very few of the updates, mostly tagged by others at volunteering events, church groups, and hiking trips. I reply to her thanking her for accepting my request and explaining that I am trying to make sense of some articles and stories I have read from the time she and Jimmy were at school together, inviting her reply or meet up for coffee.

I gulp my Chateauneuf du Pape like its Ribena rather than a 50 quid bottle of wine. I torment myself by relaying back the conversation with Mr and Mrs Finley. I must have looked so desperate asking them about Jimmy's state of mind and blurting out the newspaper headline. I could see Daphne's pained eyes as I tossed in my grenade, digging up memories of her son and then taking flight. I pour the last drops from the bottle with my cottage pie still warming in the oven. I hear a door slam next door and run to the window catching sight of Donald reversing down the drive.

The adrenaline shot is intense, the opportunity to take back control, not having to rely upon others as I put shoes on and walk over the drive to next door and tilt the plant pot. I feel around as I did before but cannot see it, I lift the plant pot and move it over to the side using the torch on my phone to look again. There is no sign of it. Damn it.

Of course, it's the weekend, no builders needing access today. What if in the future he is always home to let them in, I feel desperate, my access cut off. I need to get into the house, I need his identification to check his criminal history, and I need to be his nuisance, to play with his mind. I think of Jimmy, and I think of his shed. I walk round to the back, to his shed. The padlock fuels my anger, who locks a shed in a tiny cul-de-sac? I take a couple of steps back and stare at the scaffolding, wanting to tear it all down. His security lights are already on inside, and I notice an upstairs window open nestled in amongst the scaffolding. Can I do this?

I climb the ladder and bend under the imposing metal bar at the top, probably the same bar the builders leap over five times a day, but I am a bottle of red and four beers down. I look down at the muddy wooden plank still damp from the earlier rain and creep over to the window. I reach my hand inside to lift the catch extending as far as it will go. It still looks a tight squeeze, and the window frame is beginning to rot, I could just as easily pull the whole frame out and just step in. I hoist my left leg through, balancing on the bed beneath, then shuffle my leg across the bed, so my other leg is up tight against the outer wall, all I have to do now is lift it, and my weight will carry it through.

I pause for a second imagining I must look a complete sight sitting half in, half out of a window, doing my version of the splits on top of an old rotting window frame damp against my crotch. I stand on the bed and lift my leg in, suddenly aware all my weight is on one foot and balancing on a springy bed I crash to the floor. My drunkenness hits me as lie motionless on the floor, the soothing carpet cradling my head. My new relaxed state triggers me to jump up shaking myself from sleepiness.

The room is empty bar the single bed. I walk into his dark bedroom and empty the contents of a bottle of pills and then another, swapping the contents over without looking at the labels. One mischief down, what next? I walk around upstairs, my mind suddenly blank. Last night while lying in bed, I could not sleep for the hundreds of ideas that I had to disrupt the house, but now I can't recall a single one. I walk down the stairs and see his desk remembering I need his identification.

The lamp illuminates the contents of the drawer, and I pull out a bank statement and credit card application form that is half-filled in, importantly with his date of birth. I feel my head spinning and think back to the red wine and dinner, except I did not eat it, *shit.* I left it in the oven. Black smoke is probably filling my house now, creeping out of the windows, creating a spectacle. I rush to the door only pausing as I see his wallet on the kitchen side, I open it up and pull out his driving license and a credit card shoving them into my pocket, I open the front door, eyes focused on my house looking through the windows for any sign of flames before running back across the driveway.

The moment I open the front door the acrid smell hits me, I run straight to the kitchen and swing the oven door open, the heat hits me flush in the face causing me to spring backwards on all fours. I collapse to the floor staring down at the burnt cottage pie, a perfect metaphor for my life right now, the heat remaining etched on my face.

'Everything okay, Philip?'

The voice behind me makes me jump and snaps me out of my self-induced despair. Donald is standing in my kitchen. 'I just got home, and noticed the door was open and of course smelt the burning so rather fearing the worst I just walked in,' oh the irony, and I allow myself a chuckle in my head.

I focus back on Donald who stands over me perplexed. 'Yes, all fine thanks, just lost track of time in the bath and then-'

'But, you are not wet,' he interrupts.

Why did I say bath, why did I need to say anything? I could have just said mind your own business, get out of my house.

'I dried myself and got dressed before realising I had the oven turned on too high,' I begrudgingly elaborate before finally picking myself up.

'I always set the timer on my phone when cooking,' he says, turning to leave—my phone. My hand goes to my pocket; it is empty. I walk through to the hallway, no sign there either. The last time I remember having it was....shit! I must have left it in the upstairs room next door; when I fell off the bed, I was using it as a torch. My mind racing a million different thoughts, how can I justify myself coming into his house and going upstairs to retrieve it?

I can think of nothing. He is across the driveway; he puts his key in the door and walks in, slamming it shut behind him. What now?

A footprint, a misplaced remote control, a window left ajar, they can all be dismissed as old age forgetfulness, can be blamed on the builders if necessary, but my mobile phone sitting in his guest bedroom? I need to retrieve it.

I have entered his house twice, but this is a different ball game. I see him through the window in the kitchen, so stand and hold back, too risky now while he is moving about. I sit down outside my front door and try to formalise some sort of response if we were to come face to face inside. The only response that makes any sense is a physical one, can I do this? One right hook, left jab, boot into the body. I feel no aggression even going through these motions in my head, only fear. I stand to attention when his kitchen falls into darkness and watch him moving through his house to the living room. I edge a little closer to watch him sit down in his armchair with a tray of food and switch on the television. Ha, so he found his remote control.

This is my chance, with the television blaring out some old war film, straight in, straight out. I walk to the back of the house which is now lit up like floodlights on a sports pitch. I move slowly, hugging the wall. Above me, one room shines a white light out into the night sky, my phone torch facing upwards illuminating the room like a beacon. I climb the ladder as I did only an hour before, each step causing a noisy clunking sound, I duck again under the bar at the top, so much harder in slow motion.

I shuffle across the plank of wood unable to avoid the nuts and bolts sprinkling down to the concrete below. I stand outside the open window, determined not to repeat my mistakes of earlier but think of no other way to enter. I repeat my method, this time more slowly. I pull my second leg in as if in slow motion, sinking slowly to my knees on the bed to at least keep upright. My phone sits in the middle of the room as if a centrepiece. As I go to turn off my torch, I catch a glimpse of the bed; the single duvet ruffled and as I go in closer, stained mud from my

95

footprints. I slap away some of the dried mud and turn over the duvet taking care to straighten it out. I take my right shoe off and stand my foot on the mattress next to the pillow for leverage.

I freeze at the sound of the phone ringing. I go to my pocket in panic, holding it out in front of me. Nothing. The ringing continues with my phone in darkness. It takes an eternity for me to realise it is the house phone, and I blowout my hot breath in relief. The sound of the TV pauses, and I hear him marching to the hallway repeating his number back when answering, all the while not moving a muscle.

'No, you have the wrong bloody number, I don't care what message you got.' Donald slams the phone down.

I stay rooted to the spot, one foot on the bed the other on the floor about to be hoisted out the window. I await to hear his direction with apprehension. Still no resumption of the TV, my concern grows that he has been distracted, he could come upstairs at any moment. I reach out, pull the window in so it can't be seen as out of place if he looks out of his bedroom window—my chest heaving. I think again what my response is should the door behind me open. I still have no plan, I bow my head, half for prayer, and half to relieve some of the tension in my body. My legs are weighted, and my muscles on fire from the continued adrenaline rush. I vow here and now, if I get out safely, I will not return.

There is movement next door, in his bedroom, I did not even hear him on the stairs. My palms are clammy, my t-shirt sticking to my back, I feel sweat forming everywhere. I pray for real this time, just let me out of this one.

Louder noises, but welcome sounds of footsteps going down the stairs, the sound of gunfire from the television, a sigh of relief. I continue my climb out of the window, my leg stiff. I push the window back, leaving only a small gap, as I found it, and tiptoe along with the wood plank, down the ladder and around the house to home.

I down a pint of water, still lukewarm from the tap and immediately fill it up again. I sit down at the table, my heart slowing, my breaths lightening. I have been in some scary situations in the past. I have been mugged, I have been chased by a gang of football hooligans, and I have crashed my car; yet have never been so scared as tonight. I have never felt so vulnerable, the reality of being bang to rights if discovered. What am I doing? I keep justifying it to myself. It is for justice, for Jimmy, for all those victims not yet known. *Stay in control.* But from nowhere, the first crumbs of doubt creep into my mind, what if I am wrong and he is innocent. And if he is innocent, what does that make me?

Chapter Nineteen – 12 days after

I wake with my usual grogginess, horrible dry mouth, and more than a tinge of regret. There is no light fighting to get through the perimeter of my curtains, too early. I am sweating and search my conscious for recollections of the night before. In the drama of having to return for my phone, I had forgotten about switching Donald's pills around, having no idea what they were or therefore the possible consequences. Half of me wants to rush over there and tell him everything. I need to enter the house again, despite everything I promised myself last night, but this time to put things right.

I check my Facebook, no new friends, but I do have a message from Victoria replying to mine from last night requesting a chat. She suggests coming for a walk on the Downs this afternoon with her and a small walking group, nothing too strenuous and would give plenty of time to talk, although she is unsure if she can shed much light on whatever I am looking for. What *am* I looking for?

Donald is up and in his shed. No overdose last night then. I stand at the window and stare down at him. I wonder what he does for hours on end in there. It is detached from his house but purposely linked by paving stones. It is of a wooden structure with a door that looks reinforced and boasting a proper keyhole lock and the standard padlock you would expect on a shed. To the left of the door is a small window but covered up with a makeshift curtain from the inside, keeping prying eyes out. It looks different from when Jimmy spent hours upon hours in there. It seems more secure but also more functioning. I open the laptop and finish my application to the Criminal Record Bureau for the check on any criminal history against Donald, the SLA is 72 hours, but I may hear back sooner is the standard response.

I search through my suitcase and the scatter of my clothing over the floor. I am not a walker, so best I can do is jeans, trainers, and a Hugo Boss jacket. Stylish? Yes. Practical? Probably not. I remember my dad has some walking gear on his bed awaiting the charity shop, at least I can look the part. I squeeze into his waterproof trousers, his big brown boots with laces up to the ankles fit me surprisingly well as does his Saloman bright red windproof jacket. As I pick up my car keys, I catch sight once again of the photograph with the two boys on the moors, dressed as I am right now, walking a little in his footsteps perhaps.

I stand leaning against my car at our meeting place as if on a blind date. Although only half an hour's drive away, I have never been here before today and did not realise just how popular it was, I guess Sunday afternoon is peak walking time. Groups are beginning to gather, dogs are being leashed, and it suddenly dawns on me that I am going to struggle to recognise Victoria, everybody looks the same. The group to my left have hiking sticks, maps, lunch boxes and I even spot a flare gun in the outside pocket of a rucksack, *please god not them.*

I see Victoria on the opposite side of the car park, recognising her small orange beanie hat from an old Facebook post on her wall. I walk over to her and two others, a guy dressed in a black puffer jacket and woman dressed in a blue fleece, thankfully no hiking sticks or Kendal mint cake in sight.

'Hi Victoria,' I say with confidence, raising a wave as I walk over. Her eyes fix on me, smiling with all her face, which I find myself mirroring. As I stand in front of her, my eyes are drawn to her flawless complexion, glowing in the sun.

'Hiya Phil, please call me Vicky, only my mum calls me Victoria, this is Penny and Michael.'

We exchange small waves to each other even though standing only a metre apart. Vicky is much smaller than her two companions, she is wearing a pair of white sports trainers, blue tracksuit bottoms and a pink Nike waterproof jumper, clashing with her little beanie which stops just above her bottle-green eyes, no make-up but rosy cheeks and a continuing beaming smile.

'Just the three of us today Phil, just us die-hards, you certainly look the part.' I feel my cheeks blush as three sets of eyes look me up and down. 'I did not realise you were a serious rambler.'

I can't say I have never walked before, dressed like this looks like I am trying too hard. I also don't want to say I am kitted out in my dead dad's clothes. 'I just enjoy the fresh air, blows off a few cobwebs,' I reply, and with that, we are off. Our small group of four pale in comparison with most of the walkers boasting twenty or thirty strong clusters.

Vicky catches me studying the rucksacks passing us and calls out, 'I am glad you left your sandwiches behind Phil, I forgot to mention we make a point of stopping at the Stoneacre pub for a pint and bite to eat. I am pretty sure that is the only reason Michael tags along.'

'That and your scintillating banter Vicky,' Michael quips.

I feel at ease, and grateful I am not climbing in single file up the peak with thirty professional walkers talking about their pace and munching on energy bars.

After some polite small talk, Vicky asks me outright, 'So, what is your story Phil? Where did you disappear to?'

Although I was expecting this question, I still take a couple of breaths to compose myself.

'Well after Jimmy passed away, life was never the same. My parents split up without ever telling me as such, and I moved to Chichester with my mum. It was not so bad, much bigger than Baysworth, which suited me; being a new kid in a big town is much easier than a small one.'

'Oh wow that's tough Phil, your brother passing away, your parents splitting up and having to start a new school, sounds like a lot of pressure.'

'I was fortunate that at the time of starting school, a couple of local schools had merged into one, so another unfamiliar face was more accepted. I made some friends through playing sport, providing a welcome level playing field socially. I was not 'Phil the new kid from Baysworth,' or 'Phil, whose brother committed suicide.' I was simply Phil Jenkins, centre midfielder. I skipped Uni to focus on getting a job in Facilities Management for the council to help my mum with the bills. Then met a girl, moved to Glasgow, doing a similar job before redundancy a couple of months ago, then arrived back here to sort out my dad's house after he passed away.'

Vicky gave me a sympathetic look before clearly trying to lighten the mood. 'I bet Chichester is a lively place for a teenager, more so than Baysworth anyway.'

I chuckle at the thought of Vicky thinking Chichester as lively, but also recognise her intention placing a positive spin and inviting me to talk some more.

'As with most teenagers, I developed some well-crafted distractions for my studies. My friends and I would drink cans up at the park until we boasted enough facial hair to give us the confidence to start going to the pub, with our homemade ID, lumberjack shirts, ripped denim, and Doc Martins. The ID was not necessary, and we were already acquainted with Dave, the bar manager of the Rose & Crown through another of my vices – the bookies. You have to be 18 to place a bet, and I had been going there for a couple of years, so he did not bat an eyelid when we turned up at his pub. There was little else in the way of entertainment. I experimented a little with drugs, although to be honest, my friends were very anti, so it wasn't an option. Everybody talks about peer pressure when you are kids, but it can work positively as well. One of the best weekends was my 18th birthday when we held a big party at the Rose & Crown. The look on Dave's face, was priceless as he spotted the 'Happy 18th Birthday' banner and balloons – he had been serving us for over two years completely unaware.'

'Oh wow Phil, confessing under-age gambling, under-age drinking and experimenting with drugs, this is the worst first date.'

'Eh!' is all I can manage, although I did not need to say anything, my startled look and tense body a portrait of confusion.

'I am joking Phil, seriously its refreshingly honest that's all. So tell me, back to boring Baysworth after the bright lights of Chichester and Glasgow, how long are you sticking around for?'

How long am I sticking around for? I keep putting off the whole life plan thing, but in recent days I have started to refer to my dad's house as my house. I guess everyone needs somewhere to call home, temporary or not.

Her mention of a date, joke or not consumes my mind, and I feel unable to rid the tenseness in my body. I only wanted to meet for some information on Jimmy and suddenly feel uncomfortable giving my life story to a stranger. I need to turn the conversation from me to him.

'I am not sure at the moment. You see, I found some documents that have raised some questions about Jimmy. I want to find out more before I can think of moving on for peace of mind.'

Penny and Michael took an inquisitive glance at us, and increased their pace in front, clearly wanting no part of this in-depth conversation on a Sunday afternoon on the Dorset Moors.

'Somebody mentioned Jimmy was due to change schools. Can I ask Vicky, do you remember how Jimmy was at school? I lean in a little closer, lowering my voice. 'In particular, the weeks leading up to his suicide.'

Vicky slows her stride and glances off towards the disappearing figures of Penny and Michael. 'I liked Jimmy a lot, we partnered up for some project work at school, he was really smart. Everybody liked him, and his enthusiasm was infectious, always a bit of a joker. I remember he was football daft, he would be buzzing on Wednesday morning with the game in the afternoon, and would always come in on Thursday bragging about how many goals he scored and how we were going to win the cup.'

'And the changing schools?'

'Yes, he was going to change schools and boasted about it to everyone. It was some elite school that excelled at sports, he got a little big-headed to be honest. We all signed his shirt and said our goodbyes at the end of the term.' She smiles, recalling the tom foolery of final day of term.

I knew he loved his football, but I did not know Jimmy had been so smart. 'Please go on.'

'Then he suddenly appeared back at Baysworth after the summer holidays, and....'

I stop, fixing my eyes on hers, pleading with my hands. *Out with it, tell me.* 'And what Vicky?'

She bowed her head. 'And only when he came back, he was a different person.'

I need more than that. 'Different in what way Vicky? Tell me.' She turns her head away at my rising voice. 'I am sorry Vicky, I am just trying to build a picture of his state of mind, it might be important.'

'I understand Phil, but it was a long time ago, and your mind can play tricks, memories get jumbled together.'

'Anything you can tell me will help, no matter how vague, how was he different?'

Her eyes reluctantly meet mine, the spark withdrawn, her lips pursed.

'In every way.'

Vicky let out a defeated sigh as if her persona reflects that of Jimmy's. 'He lost interest in football, dropped out of the team, he lost interest in lessons, in life. He hardly spoke to anyone; he never ate in the canteen with us; in fact, he never ate full stop. He became so skinny and bony. A few people teased him about his new school rejecting him and having to come back, there may have been a fight at one stage. He lost his friends. I remember he used to just sit on his own out in the playing field, skipping lessons.'

I run the palms of my hands over my face, struggling to process all of this, how his life slipped away and how it was allowed to slip away. 'Surely, though, the teachers did not allow him to skip lessons?'

'I think it was only History lessons.'

'Tell me.' My hands tensing in my pockets.

'He would sit outside on the field, opposite the classroom, in full view of everyone, almost taunting the teacher. I remember some of the other guys thought it unfair how he was allowed to get away with it.'

I count in my head and take steadying breath before asking the question, already knowing the answer. 'Who was his teacher?'

'Mr Lloyd.'

I close my eyes at hearing his name again, his image flashing before me. 'What did he do about it?'

'That's just it, nothing. He would let Jimmy do whatever he wanted. Like Jimmy had some hold over him. I thought it strange because History was always his favourite subject, and we used to joke that if we partnered with Jimmy in History, we would be guaranteed an A grade. He was a proper teachers' pet, always having one-to-one chats with Mr Lloyd, even at lunchtime or in the playground after school.'

The building anger takes me by surprise even though it was the answer I expected, maybe also hoped for, some clarity at least, a clear direction.

As we start our climb on the moors, the silence between us grows uncomfortable, I turn to Vicky and notice a creeping vulnerability, I want to take her in my arms and thank her. I need to offer some sort of explanation for my impatience, easier than an apology.

'The documents I mentioned that I found were some old newspaper articles when I was clearing out my dad's things. They were about the investigations into sexual abuse at Baysworth, and they were talking about closing down the school. That's why I am so keen to know more. Do you remember that?'

'Of course, I remember, we had left school by then, and I was at college, but it was still a big deal. We all reckoned it was Mr Bradshaw, or Baggy Bradshaw as we called him because he always carried a big rucksack with him wherever he went, with kiddie toys, we reckoned after reading the headlines. One of the guys thought it could have been Loitering Lloyd because he used to loiter around the boys changing rooms after his PE lessons.'

Bastard, I did not know he taught PE. 'Did anyone get arrested? Were any of the pupils named?'

'It was weird. It was a huge thing, everybody talking about it, talk of the school closing, talk of everyone needing to be interviewed by the police, and then...'

'Then what Vicky?'

'Then, nothing. The school opened as normal, and it was never spoken about again.'

I roll the dice one more time. 'Do you think it could have happened, covered up maybe to protect the teachers?'

'I don't know, to be honest, they all returned to work the next day, nobody suddenly retired ten years early or suddenly got transferred.'

Vicky suddenly grabs me by the arm, her mouth open. 'Do you think that's what might have happened to Jimmy?'

'I don't know, but *something* happened to him.'

The sight of the Stoneacre pub is a welcome sight providing

some light relief to us both.

We have a couple of pints in the pub. I have forgotten how nice beer is with company in a pub rather than from a can at my kitchen table. Caroline always used to say I preferred my own company, but truth is I like hanging out with people. It's just Caroline's friends I didn't like hanging out with, occasionally showing my face only at Caroline's insistence. I found them so fake. Always showing off about their latest purchases, their exotic holidays, and new cars. It was boring.

The Caroline I knew at University would have hated them too with her socialist tendencies. She never really knew I also disliked her university friends as well, but for very different reasons, I masked it well. I guess, the older we become, the more we value time, and I grew less tolerant and cared a little less about what others thought.

Having a couple of pints with Vicky, Penny and Michael is nice, a relaxed conversation, nobody trying to be something they are not, aside from me and my attire. Vicky is a real homegirl, while most others have fled to London or beyond chasing the bright city lights, Vicky lives across the street from her parents and sees them every day. She has worked for the same small family firm of accountants since college and as she puts it, gets her social fix from the church and a few clubs like this walking one. She comes across as very measured and unassuming in every sense. I feel comfortable being open with her, knowing there is no judgement, but then again, I have nothing to lose.

As we set off again, warmed by our roast dinners and lighter topics of conversation, Vicky asks me about the girl I mentioned and where does she feature in this open timeline of being down in Dorset. I tell her the truth; we have separated, the pressures of trying and failing to start a family, the demands of maturing into different people, and maturing in different directions. I feel obliged to ask her about her relationship status and choose to dress it up under pretence equally. 'How does your other half feel about living so close to your parents?'

'No time for men, mum says I am married to the church,' laughing nervously.

I mention my meeting with the local vicar and the uplifting effect it had on me.

'He is good, we were all a little wary at first, Reverend Davies had been at the Parish for twenty years before him, and nobody likes change, especially the Parish at Baysworth. You should come next Sunday morning for service if you are still here. Or if feeling brave, listen to us bell ringing on Tuesday nights, a cup of tea to the first 800 through the door.' I return her smile.

As we reach the car park, Vicky turns to me with a look of carefulness, *or is it sympathy?* 'I am sorry I could not give you the answers you were looking for.'

'No, it's been helpful thanks. Hey, one final thing, was there anything out of the ordinary at school the day before he committed suicide, a fight or an argument?'

Vicky pauses and looks me straight in the eye. 'I don't know Phil, and I didn't see him. It was half term that week.'

I feel the blood draining from my face, through my body, weakening my knees.

'What is it? Are you OK Phil? What have I said?'

I swallowed hard to generate just enough saliva to answer. 'Could there have been any school events that week?'

Vicky shook her head slowly. 'Definitely not, my mum ran a church activity week there during half term, it was so weird being the only kid in school during a holiday. Jimmy's funeral was the same day as the first day back.'

'Vicky thank you so much, it was lovely to meet you and hear your recollections of Jimmy, I appreciate it, and you have given me such clarity. I have to get home now but will see you again, I hope.'

As I turn and walk towards my car, I blow hard, the escaping breath held inside me since the mention of half-term. My fingernails dig into my palms as my fist clenches. The alarm bell is ringing loud and clear in my head as I sit at the wheel.

Chapter Twenty – 12 days after

I sit squeezing the steering wheel of my car watching the many Hunter boots being kicked off and cleaned of their mud before being thrown in the boot of spotlessly clean Range Rovers. Conversations throughout the car-park are already turning to tomorrow's commute and to-do list in the office. I continue the breathing exercise I learnt from the therapy sessions that Caroline insisted I attend. Three seconds in, seven seconds out, swapping the angry gravelled voice in my head to a whisper. I drive purposely slowly out of the car park, pausing and raising a sympathetic wave to a distressed woman chasing after her loose dog running in front of me.

I turn on the radio as my mind pieces together the past to what Vicky has just revealed, wanting to piece together *that* week. I remember Dad and Jimmy had argued. Mum and I on the peripheral as they sparred with one another before Jimmy stood up, throwing down his cutlery onto his plate, a splatter of gravy on the tablecloth. Jimmy was pleading to give up football as if it had been the fight of his life. Mum sat mute, eyes fixed on her plate. I waited for my dad to yell his instruction to sit back down, but instead stood toe to toe against him, shouting 'WHY?'

Jimmy had said he was slipping behind with his schoolwork.

Yet, what had Vicky just told me, that Jimmy's grades had always been excellent. I pressed my foot a little harder on the accelerator. Jimmy had said he didn't have friends on the team but didn't Vicky just say he was popular? I chewed my lip, a pinching pain forcing my foot harder against the accelerator. What else did Jimmy and Dad say in their verbal spar? Jimmy claimed he was tired, but I had already taken over his paper round, and dammit, Vicky just told me Jimmy had boundless energy on match days.

The music on the radio gets louder, the beat faster. Dad had stood in front of him at the dining table, pleading now. *'It could your future, a scholarship, make something of your life'.* I can see him now, the image of Jimmy, eyes brimming with unshed tears, all colour sucked dry from his cheeks as he calmly replied *'What life.'*

I barrel down the road lined with shops and people now, only noticing the man waving his fist in my rear view mirror, standing in the middle of the street, the Zebra crossing disappearing out of my sight. *Why did he hate football of a sudden? Maybe it wasn't football, maybe it was* the showers. *Oh my God Jimmy, my brother…*You can't explain that at the dinner table. No-one can account for the showers, apart from maybe 'Loitering Lloyd.' *That animal. That barbaric animal.* I see the whites of my knuckles strapped to the steering wheel.

Vicky said Jimmy skipped History, yet it had been his favourite subject, top grades she had said. All these years and I'd never known of the most telling details of my brother's life and pain. *He was right: what life?* I pound the wheel with my fists with a ferocity that I beg will undo the past.

A woman jumps to the pavement dragging her child close to her chest, her face ashen white with horror, tins rolling from her shopping bag. Her stare strikes through me like lightning, my teeth gritting in defiance. And all the time Lloyd let him to do whatever he wanted, like Jimmy had something over him.

I turn into my street, my anger, frustration and powerlessness rippling up and colliding inside me, turning me into a seething seeker of revenge. I want to hurt him bad. I want him to be standing on his drive, head down focused on his flowers, rising just in time to see my telling face behind the wheel, for our eyes to meet knowingly. I want to see the panic in his body, his eyes popping and legs shuffling nowhere. I want him to feel the pain before my car hits him, and I want to watch in slow motion his lifeless body flinging in the air, catching the briefest glimpse of my smile and mouthing *JIMMY*, before crashing against the house, sliding to the ground.

I turn the final corner, my eyes hungrily seeking him, heart dropping like lead when I see the driveway empty.

I try to bury it, but there is no grave deep enough to hold my fears. I slam the car door and run into the house straight up the stairs, two at a time, and pull out my dad's box of papers. I grab hold of the separated pile and pull the paperclip off and flick through at pace. *There.* Found it. Booking confirmation for Mr Jenkins from 19th February to 23rd February 1986, 2-bed cottage, Apollo Cottages, Brixham. Our usual holiday booking, but no cleaning receipt this time, because we never made it there. We should have arrived on 19th February 1986. Vicky was right, it was half term that week, and I have vague memories of packing a bag on that fateful morning. My mouth is so dry. Jimmy was not going to school, and he had no intention of going to school, we were going on holiday. Instead, he put on his school uniform to hang himself in our garage, his only escape.

Message received Jimmy, loud and clear.

I charge out of the house and across the driveway. I bang on his door ignoring the bell, my anger only building as I wait for it to open. I bang again, louder. No answer. In my rage, I had not even noticed the car still absent from the drive. I walk around the house; all windows are secure this time. I wish I had paint to scroll over his house, to tell the world who he really is, and what he did. The fire inside me rages, lacing my veins and engulfing my spine. I pick up a rock and hurl it through the bedroom window. The glass shatters, leaving a hole amongst daggers, an instant release.

I go back inside and look for a beer and find only an empty fridge at *the worst possible time.* I stare at the internal door to the garage. I still have not found the key to this door or the outer one. I have had enough of searching, waiting for email replies, waiting to meet people, and for the remaining pieces to complete my jigsaw. I kick the door hard with the sole of my shoe just above the handle. I kick a second time and feel some movement. My third kick is rewarded with a crash.

A surge of power goes straight through me at the sight of the door crashing open. The escaping cold air blows into my face and I taste its staleness. I reach out and find the light switch hidden behind dust and cobwebs. The dim light only reveals the emptiness of the space, nothing apart from a few leaves that have slipped under the garage door. I tentatively step onto the concrete floor as if it were a frozen lake, seeing the image of my parents laying on the floor, their world, our world, blown to pieces. The smell of dampness hanging in the air. In a shadowed corner, I spot a single bottle of whiskey. I understand its purpose, its symbolism. I take it back to the kitchen and open it, pouring myself a glass and walk back to the garage raising the glass and toast, *'to my big brother, I will put things right,'* and down it. The warmth hits the back of my throat. I cough and take a sharp breath through my nose and mouth, tasting it again. I return to the kitchen, dropping some ice into my glass to take the edge off the bitterness. I slump into my dad's armchair, staring at the blank television screen, providing an unwelcome reflection of my anger. Whom I have become.

My mind fills with haunting images of what might have gone on. How Lloyd would loiter around the changing rooms after Jimmy's football, all those little private chats at school, the promise of good grades? All those hours spent in the shed, filling his head with war stories like some kind of hero that he did not have at home. I don't understand why Jimmy didn't say something, why he didn't fight back? I know so little about all of this. But children are vulnerable and muted by fear, which is why the media is full of men years later speaking up.

I think about Donald calling in favours from DI Mayne, his brother from the Lodge, how brotherhood was deemed more important than justice as the police turned a blind eye and shot down the investigation. They are as guilty as Donald. I notice my hand shaking, a trembling rage.

I reach down for the bottle, my medicine, nearly half down, and it has hardly touched the sides. I must have been drinking in a trance, slowly numbing my senses. As I stand, I feel its full effect. I sway from side to side, my head like a lead weight, my eyes swivelling to the back of my head, unable to focus.

I open my front door and stare at his house. Through my gritted teeth, I mumble my hate, my lust to inflict pain swelling. I reach down to pick up a half-brick sitting in my flower bed and throw it hard against his house, causing me to stumble.

It misses the window scuffing the brick wall, but has whetted my appetite once again. I freeze momentarily and smile at the sight of his car back on the drive, and my mind goes to him finding the smashed window, maybe calling police friends. I think of him and DI Mayne as I stride over to his car and kick the wing mirror clean off.

'COME ON DONALD, COME ON,' I shout, standing with an exaggerated wide stance, my chest heaving, and arms spread wide. My adrenaline is pumping, now or never, I choose to fight.

I smile with a warped pride as my cries go unanswered, I want him to hide from me, to fear me, to feel how Jimmy felt and then I will strike him, right hook, left jab, kick to his stomach. I walk round to the back of the house, scouring the garden for another brick to fire straight into his lounge window. I imagine the glass shattering at his feet, and I want to see him scared. My eyes search for him. I don't see him, I don't see anything. A huge dust sheet extended right across the scaffolding blocking eyes into the house, but then also blocking any eyes out.

I seek my next move. I stare at his shed as I have done a hundred times in the past fortnight. I take a couple of steps to the door and kick it hard, leaving it hanging by its hinges as if by a thread. I kick again at the hinges, and the door slams flush to the floor like an open drawbridge, a surge of power filtering through me. I flick the light switch which illuminates four spotlights sunken into a garnished wooden ceiling.

It is like the Tardis, much bigger inside than outside, fitted out like a Scandinavian log cabin and furnished like a showcase kids' room in Ikea. I stand in awe taking in my surreal surroundings. A small flat-screen television on one wall with DVD player and Xbox below with two mini reclining armchairs facing. A mini-fridge in the corner, a trendy red one with a metal handle and a fashionable Dyson fan, one of those bladeless ones that make you want to put your hand through. On the wall are two narrow mirrors and framed pictures everywhere, of show jumping, of popstars, of the Eiffel Tower, of youth. A small bookcase with pop and fashion magazines. The place even smells like candy. Nothing looks out of place, apart from a dirty green plastic box tucked away in the corner. It is full of rusty old tins of paint and oil, old paintbrushes with solid brushes, half-empty bottles of weed killer, varnish and white spirit.

I pick up the white spirit and push the sticky top-down, then to the right, with every turn soaking my finger and thumb in the greasy colourless fluid. The bottle immediately bends in my hand as the air is released. I pour the remains of the bottle over the two chairs tossing the empty bottle to the floor. I reach down into the green box once again and pull out a small box of safety matches. I push open the small cardboard box from within, pulling out four matches, striking them purposely along the sandpaper of the matchbox. They alight as one with an instant spark against the friction, and for a second, I am mesmerised by the tiny inferno between my fingers, a little dark wisp of smoke floating upward. Holding such power between my fingers. I lower it carefully to touch the small pool of fluid sitting on the chair which immediately ignites and spreads, following the fluid path all over the seat like a small river weaving through a valley. I light another match and toss it on the second chair, the small flame curls around the match, igniting much slower and confined to just one corner, the deep orange flame twinkling before rising and transforming to a deep yellow, the chair melting slowly as the fire spreads.

The flames flicker before me, the oppressive heat suffocating my face and smoke flowing upwards hitting the ceiling and blanketing all the walls. I take a couple of steps backwards out of the doorframe, the fresh evening air cleansing me. The small curtain covering the window catches a loose cinder and catches fire instantly. I take another couple of steps backwards, keeping my eyes fixed on the multiplying grey smoke chasing me out of the door. The crackling is deafening in the quiet of this night.

The scene changes before my eyes as the smoke turns to a thick black fog. Flames begin to eat their way through the shed wall where the green box sits, engulfing its shell. Rising high in the night sky and dancing to the tune of the wind, bouncing out of control, snarling and biting at the huge sheet covering the scaffolding. Suddenly I feel small and helpless, all control and power emptied of me. The black fog is surrounding me like an evil spirit, filling my lungs, awakening me from my rage.

I fall to my knees, blinking hard to rid my eyes of the poison. I bow my head, clenching my fists tight, willing to wake up in my bed. I hear Caroline's voice next to me, sounding disappointed at first, asking me questions and then angrier, screaming now, *take control*, my wake up call.

I leap to my feet and run towards the scaffolding, grabbing the dust sheet and pulling it hard. My eyes flood with tears at the impenetrable task and then drown in fear as it catches alight. I look back to the shed behind me engulfed in flames, ash beginning to rain down.

I scan the garden and pick up a broom from the wet lawn and turn to the dust sheet whacking it hard, beating the fire down. The broom slices open the fragile embers of the sheet with chunks falling to the ground giving me a sudden clear view into the living room window. I see Donald asleep in his chair, the reflection of the television on his glasses and I start banging hard on the window.

He wakes with a startle and his eyes fix first on me then on the bright orange glow behind me, he rises to his feet and opens the patio door, eyes still fixed on the shed.

'What the hell,' he screams above the blaring noise from the television.

'Donald, call the fire brigade and then get out of the house.'

He turns and shuffles to the hallway, and I remember having seen a fire extinguisher in his kitchen fixed to the wall above his fridge. I run in, past Donald dialling frantically and grab it, running upstairs to the spare room, I jump on the bed and out of the same window I had used before. I stand on the platform, gripping the extinguisher hard, firing the foam downwards onto the flames, suffocating them until all I can see at the bottom of the sheet is a ring of dirty foam.

I jump over the metal bar and skip down the steps two at a time firing at the shed with the remaining foam until it shoots out only air and bubbles—the foam slides off the walls revealing a charcoaled black shell. The extinguisher is ingrained into the palm of my hand as I try and let go. I peel my fingers one by one off the black metal handle. Tears fill my eyes, relief it is over but already drowning in guilt.

I stagger back in the house through the patio doors, Donald stands opposite me with fright in his eyes. 'Philip, Philip, are you OK, I am so sorry I don't know what could have happened.'

I am standing next to his sofa chair but fall to my knees. My mind contemplates just for a second if I can sit here and accept his accolades, be the hero. But how could I live with myself? I could face charges, and what credibility would a liar, an arsonist, an attempted murderer have in proving another man's guilt?

'It was me, Donald.' My voice alien to me.

'It was me that set fire to your shed. I only meant to frighten you. I did not know it would spread so quickly.'

Like a naughty schoolboy, I don't take my eyes off the carpet, so I don't see his fist swinging at me, striking my temple, the shock knocking me over rather than the ferocity. 'You burned down my shed,' he snorts standing over me.

Red mist explodes within me, I jump up and charge him backwards with my shoulder in his gut and my arms wrapped around him, gathering pace as he stumbles back onto the bookshelf not letting go of me. I wriggle an arm free and put in a couple of digs to his stomach. Still, he holds onto me, allowing no room for a proper swing.

'You killed my brother,' I shout to fuel my flurry of punches into his ribs. I wrestle free and stand up, taking a step back ready to launch at him properly this time. He lies at the foot of his bookcase, his face pure white, looking suddenly old and vulnerable. I tighten my fists, I grit my teeth, but he just lies there staring at me like a frightened animal trying to make sense of it all, his eyes lost.

'What do you mean, Philip? I did not kill your brother. He committed suicide.'

I crouch down, my face in his. 'And why was that Donald? You were abusing him,' showing him my clenched fist. 'You killed him, I read the papers about the police investigation, you killed him, I know about you.' I don't recognise my voice, a shrill fuelled by emotion, an outpouring of relief rather than aggression.

I slump down to the carpet, my knees giving way, the

enormous weight I have been carrying lifted, all my moves played, blood draining from my body.

I hear the sirens. I imagine the neighbours gathering outside or at their windows, a scene building. The sirens are getting louder, fight or flight. I do not want any more regrets, I need to buy myself some time, and I stand to leave.

'Philip wait. I would never do anything like that. I was fond of Jimmy. I would never have done that or anything to hurt him. You need to look closer to home. You were too young to understand Jimmy, and too young to know who your dad really was? Do you even know why your mum just upped and left like that?' Donald spoke through gritted teeth, hiding behind his outstretched arm, surrendering, his eyes masked by fear.

My eyes are diverted, red and blue lights dancing all over the walls. Fight or Flight. I run out the patio door to the back garden and over the fence, not stopping, not looking back.

Chapter Twenty-One – 13 days after

I lie awake, much like the other nights. My conscience fights for attention against my memory. There's a pungent smell of smoke on my hands, on my clothes, and now on the bedsheets. My eyes so dry. The guilt is suffocating. The image of the shed burned to the ground already haunting me. The flames, only the width of the scaffolding away from the house, and Donald lying on the floor. He must have thought I had gone mad.

I shut these images down, only for Donald's parting shots to echo in my head. The *'need to look closer to home'* and how I was *'too young to understand Jimmy'* and *'never knew who my dad was.'* The last statement is the hardest. I don't know if he meant figuratively or literally. *Was he not my dad at all?* It would explain the distance he put between us after mum and I left, I was the child in the relationship, yet I could count on one hand how many times he came to visit, and I repaid this apathetic attitude in my later life. If he was not my dad, then what about Jimmy? I always thought we were similar, same interests and all, but maybe I was intentionally following in his footsteps by way of a tribute. I wander around the house, lost in my own life, drowning in doubt.

I was 11 years old when he died. Of course I did not understand him, but then neither did my parents, and if they did, they gave nothing away. Regardless, Donald knew my dad was hiding something, something so great it had something to do with Jimmy's suicide and maybe mum leaving him. I believed him when he said he would never hurt Jimmy, I saw it in the whites of his eyes.

What if Jimmy wasn't escaping Donald's hold on him? What if he was escaping the holiday with us, the holiday with dad? In my mind, I keep going back to my childhood, wanting to dismiss this. Examining scene by scene, remembering it, turning it over, and looking for clues. My memory is blurred, photographs and stories I heard is all I have.

I stare at the window although I do not have to open the curtain to see the charcoaled remains of the shed and burnt sheet scrawled across the lawn. The mud covering the bottom of my jeans prompts the memory of me hiding in the woods last night after running from the scene. I crouched behind a tree, like an animal for hours, expecting to see a line of torches and sniffer dogs hunting down me down. I sheepishly snuck back to the house in the early hours, only when I was sure it was completely void of life.

I can hear voices outside, a car door closing igniting my speeding heartbeat. I prepare myself for the sight of a police car and officers walking to my door. I have no answers. I pull the curtain and breathe a sigh of relief as I watch the builders next door. They are knocking on Donald's door; I tense, waiting to catch sight of him again. They bang again but no answer, they look under the plant pot, but I know there is nothing waiting for them. The older guy holds his phone against his ear and starts to throw his arms up in the air. If Donald is not in the house, where is he? And why did he not leave the key?

I go downstairs and put the kettle on. As I pass the front

window, one of the builder's talks on the phone, nodding only to himself. I open the window to try and listen, his usual boisterous tone frustratingly is turned right down. I need to know if it is Donald on the other end of the phone. I open the door and sheepishly wander over.

'Hi there,' I say unconvincingly. 'I live just next door here, is there no sign of Donald today?'

The same older man turns around, his face badly pock marked and boasting a scar on his chin, he looks me up and down. 'No mate, no sign, and we have to get the rendering done today before the new windows arrive, he was the one pushing for us to be finished by Wednesday.'

'Finished by Wednesday?' I repeat.

'Yea mate, rendering today, new double-glazed windows in tomorrow and Wednesday we give a coat of paint, and we move onto the next job. Problem being, with him not around and that, we will have to push everything back.' He checks his watch as people do when talking about any timeline, minute, hour or day.

Donald was telling the truth about it being only a small job, all this scaffolding for some new windows and painting. I tune back into our conversation and interrupt. 'There was an incident last night, a fire in his back garden, he probably left in a hurry and forgot about you guys, what do you need access to the house for?'

He points his eyes to the sky holding his hand to his chin and glances to his colleagues. 'What every man needs, tea, biscuits and a piss now and then, oh and in our case hot water to mix the plaster.'

'I can do that.'

Suddenly, I am back in my kitchen making four cups of

steaming hot tea but know it will take a great deal more than this to make it up to Donald, assuming I ever get the chance.

I sit down with my tea and stare at the one photograph of my dad in the house on a walking trip with the two teenage boys. I stare hard at my dad. Why not pictures of us? Could he really have driven Jimmy to such despair?

I keep receiving fleeting glimpses of a very different upbringing for us. I think hard about my childhood here, in this house. Vicky talked about the change in Jimmy, but there was also a change in my dad that summer before his death. We used to spend our weekends together as a family. When Jimmy got home from his paper round, we would sit down for breakfast together and plan our day. Jimmy always wanted to go to the zoo or the lido, I was happiest at the beach, and if mum or dad got a vote, it would be for visiting a town somewhere. Saturday night Jimmy and I could choose our dinner, usually chicken nuggets and microchips in front of the television. We had our routines on a Sunday too, but that meant mum and I shopping or doing some crafts together. Dad and Jimmy would be out the door straight after his paper round for his football match. Playing for the County meant some long drives to Hampshire or Sussex, and we wouldn't see them until the evening. If there was no game, they would drive over to Bournemouth for training.

Things changed gradually rather than a big bang. Jimmy started staying home alone on Saturdays, and I assumed because he was old enough to do so. He also handed down his paper round to me that summer, a combination of him being too tired for early mornings and my coming of age to start earning my own money. When Jimmy gave up football both at school and for his club, it meant Sundays had no routine or purpose. Mum and I continued our thing, but dad went stir-crazy, not knowing what to do with himself and even occasionally went to support the team even though Jimmy was not playing. Eventually, they asked him to stop.

I feel myself getting more agitated, too many questions and not enough answers. I send another request for subject access to ACRO to identify any information held on the Police National Computer (PNC) for my dad. I want to do the same for Jimmy but cannot find any identification for him, anywhere. There is no paperwork, no birth certificate, no old passport, no library card, not even a cycling proficiency certificate.

When I cleared out my mum's possessions, I found only paperwork relating to me and had assumed Jimmy's was kept in this house, after all, why would you need a birth certificate or papers for the deceased?

I search in my dad's bedroom, looking in places where he would not want things found. At the back of his cupboard, the bottom of his sock drawer, behind his desk and under his bed. All I see is dust and old coins. I sit down on his bed, refusing to believe he only has one photograph in the whole house, of two random faces and none of Jimmy or me. I can think of no rational reason why.

Phoning Donald is a risk on so many different levels. He will be furious with me, and no doubt will be seeking justice for what I have done, maybe even question how I have his mobile number, but it is a risk I need to take. I find his old phone bill in my room and dial the number. It goes to straight to voicemail, and I decide not to leave a message. The builder from next door yells a greeting as he walks in the house holding three empty cups, 'Hello neighbour, any chance of a refill?' I put the kettle on, glad for the distraction.

He wanders nosily around my downstairs and stands in front of the broken internal door leading to the garage that I kicked down only last night. 'Eh up,' he says, 'someone has a temper on him I see.' I shuffle uncomfortably, not quite ready to tell some builder my life story and how it arrived at me having to kick down a door in my deceased dad's house.

'The lock was broken.' I offer, protesting my innocence against his grinning smile.

'Bet it gives a terrible draft, I can put a temporary solution up if you like, take some of that plywood you have stacked on the beams up there,' pointing to the garage ceiling. 'I could just cut it and block the frame for you, no charge apart from a cup of tea or four.'

'Ok thanks that would be good.' Good to block out the images I see every time I pass.

He disappears to his van and returns a few moments later with a saw and ladder, positioning it under the garage beams. A couple of laboured steps up and he is wrestling with a big piece of plywood.

'Hey mate, come and grab the other end will you.' He pushes it out from the grasp of the beams and tilts it downward, sliding it slowly towards my outstretched arms. As it drops towards me, I notice a dark shape sliding along the top of it heading straight for me, with my arms holding the wood all I can do is turn my head as it hits me on the side of my face.

'Shit, sorry I didn't realise something was stored on top.' He gabs the wood from my arms as I hold the offending item. A cardboard box, big enough for a toaster, too small for a microwave, taped up but with scars to show it has been opened and secured many times before. Well and truly hidden out of sight in the beams of a locked garage.

Chapter Twenty-Two – 13 days after

I take the box upstairs away from the prying eyes and the running commentary of the builder. In contrast to the top of the beams and plywood which hid it, there is little dust on it. I slice open the brown masking tape and gingerly open the cardboard flaps. I need both hands to lift out the stack of photographs, some secured in frames, most loosely thrown together which escape my grasp with ease and spill onto the bed.

The photographs are of all shapes and sizes, some boasting a reddish-brown sepia tone, but mostly in black and white. All presented within a delicate white border, damaged by creases and stains, frayed and curled at the edges. Staring up at me are different faces, each expressionless, and carrying the same worn look. They are from a different era. Nobody is posing or wanting admiration. They are there to be read, each carrying a story. I look hard, wanting to recognise some of the subjects. I pull one close, a well-dressed lady, smiling at the camera in front of a line-up of other women, each sporting the same exaggerated hairstyle. It could be my dad's mother, much taller and younger than my only reference which was a picture in her later years that sat by the telephone, draped in pearls with a feather boa holding a lit Sobranie.

Eccentric till the day she died, he used to say.

Another picture shows a group of men outside a factory, sporting the same crew cut hairstyle and lined up like a team photo. I hold closer to me a different picture, grainy in quality and fainter in brightness. A row of houses, grass verges and a street empty of cars. Standing in the centre is a boy holding up a bike too big for him with two girls looking on. This could be my dad.

Nestling on top of a glass frame is a thin and tattered envelope, the weight transferring to the bottom corner as I pick it up. I pull out a polished bronze medal. It has a four-pointed star nestled underneath a crown, about 50mmm in height. It sits comfortably in the palm of my hand, but its weight is noticeable. The obverse has two crossing swords with blades pointing upwards set within a wreath of oak leaves. Inscribed on a banner across the blades is '1914-1915.' Above the crown is a half-inch diameter ring that would have held a ribbon. I keep my palm flat and still, staring down at history, willing for its story to be told. I flick through the old photographs once again, finding no reference to an army uniform.

I heard only about my grandad's job in the factory, his gambling and his womanising. It does not add up. *Where did this come from?* And then the image hits me. Of Donald's study, and the frames on the wall, the collection of medals and badges. His endless stories of the war come flooding back. He spoke with pride and passion that any son would have, had it been their father. I remember the empty display case. Something was once there, taking pride of place, but now had been discarded into a desk draw, through guilt and regret from losing it. *Or having it stolen.* My cheeks flame red.

Whatever happened between my dad and Donald in the past, culminated in him making a calculated decision to take from him, and not for monetary gain, but to cause the maximum amount of distress. How could he have been so callous? But then Donald called it; I didn't know who my dad really was.

I pick up the box of remaining photographs, and poise to throw it hard against the wall out of anger and fear for what I may find next. I hold it above my head and take some deep breaths and think about Jimmy. It is Jimmy that I want answers for, my worry is that I will have to reveal who my dad was to find them. I push the old black and white photographs to one side and begin to sort through more recent pictures, many faded in colour and presented in cheap frames.

The first picture is of my mum and dad, myself and Jimmy. We are sitting at a table in a restaurant, my dad with a brown shirt, mum in a flowery dress, Jimmy with an Arsenal football shirt. I am sporting a Karate kid t-shirt, we all had napkins on our heads and beaming smiles. We look like a family.

There are a couple of others of dad and friends, work colleagues, and teammates from cricket. In amongst the pictures, almost hidden, is an invoice looking entirely out of place amongst the photographs. The headed paper reads '*Master & Taylor Solicitors*'. My eyes scan to the bottom, to the total fee of £17,211, for services simply labelled '*legal representation*'. It is dated September 1985. That is a lot of money in those days, and as with all events around this time, I work out how far away from Jimmy's death, just seven months. I Google the solicitor's name but find no reference.

I leave the invoice to one side promising to return to it and continue with the pile of photographs, becoming brighter in colour but no more familiar. My dad holding a young child, with hair much blonder than either Jimmy or I ever had. The hair flops into his eyes, his skin pale, and he is wearing only a pair of blue shorts. Another one with the same child, though in his arms this time, and another with him on his knee, all taken on different days but across a similar timeframe. The child looks about four or five years old. My dad is maybe around forty.

There are lots of pictures of the same boy standing alone looking straight at the camera, in parks, on the beach, in gardens, in a restaurant, on a sofa, on a bed. One of the pictures is of the boy naked, holding a towel above his head in a room I do not recognise. Other photographs show a different child with longer blonde hair, similar age, similar pictures, and the same locations. A final couple of pictures are mixed in perspective. The children are together this time and further from the camera, more natural-looking like they did not know the picture was being taken. My clammy hands set the photos down. The saliva has gone from my mouth and my mind racing with possible explanations: none realistic, and all demanding further explanation.

I remember the police visiting the house daily in the days and weeks after Jimmy's death, hushed voices and closed doors again. It is alien to see pictures of my dad with other children, *young* children. And the invoice from solicitors, legal representation for or from what? I sit at the window; the time has escaped me and sky darkening outside. Again I think back to my fourteen years we lived here together, my mind searching for clues. Maybe Jimmy knew something, and maybe my mum knew something. Neither are here to ask. But Donald knows something, and even Marie from the children's home knows something.

I think back to how coy she was when we spoke, and suggest-ing a meeting face to face, outside of the children's home. I am meeting her tomorrow, but this cannot wait. I call Camwell lodge and ask to speak with Marie urgently. My heart sinks when the lady on the phone tells me she has left for the day and she is off tomorrow. I have to think fast.

'Can you give me her home number? I know she is off tomorrow; I am meeting her for coffee, but now I can't make it, and I do not have her number to let her know.'

'I will pass the message on that you wish to cancel your meeting.'

'No, wait. Can you please just contact her and tell her to call me urgently, and if for any reason you can't speak to her, I will meet her as planned tomorrow, it is important that I do.'

'So you can now meet her tomorrow.'

The lady on the phone sounds confused, I think she got the message, I just hope I have not scared Marie off meeting me, though I could not fault her, I did seem very desperate.

I redial Donald's number, straight to voicemail. I have to think of Donald as an ally now, someone who can unlock the truth. *Stay in control.* But this is purely based on his denial, his denial while lying at my feet in his house. He was desperate. As quick as my faith rises, doubts set in as I think back to the contents of his suitcase. If he can hide his sexuality and lifestyle for so long, he can lie to my face, especially as I was in his home having just set fire to his shed. He would have been terrified.

I bury my head in my hands, regret for being so naïve. If I cannot ask him again directly, I can ask someone who knows him well. I feel myself getting desperate, throwing caution to the wind, I google DI Peter Mayne and pump my fist to find him listed here in Baysworth. I need to speak with him, and it needs to be face to face so I can look him in the eye and find the truth about the police investigation into the school. I put on a smart shirt to increase the chances of him opening the door to a stranger and jump in the car.

When I researched DI Mayne before there were pictures of him and attributing quotes on various investigations around the school abuse scandal, I thought he looked quite old back then. I pray he is still alive and of a sound mind.

I pull up at a big detached house directly opposite the Wagon & Horses pub on the outskirts of Baysworth. It is a small neighbourhood with a well-kept green, permanent bunting on the village hall, duck pond, and posters advertising a dog show. It is a picture-perfect English hamlet, full of retired city folk and those on a generous police pension.

The doorbell chimes only once, the sound of a gong. A man my age, but bigger build and smartly dressed opens the door and greets me with apprehension.

'Hi, I am sorry to disturb you, I am looking to speak with Peter Mayne, and this was the address listed,' I say keeping eye contact.

'That's me.'

It is not worth calling his bluff or playing games, so I am direct, 'I think Peter is a little older, a retired DI at Baysworth?'

'Oh sorry, Peter is my father, Peter Mayne Senior, I am his son. My father resides at the retirement home in Tolworth, about ten miles away. What do you want with him?'

I freeze for a second, wrapping my brain for a feasible explanation of why a stranger might want to talk to a retired Policeman. I can think of only one thing we have in common.

'We have a mutual acquaintance, Donald Lloyd. I am his neighbour and just wanted to let Peter know about an incident last night, which resulted in Donald being taken to hospital. I am letting all of his Mason brothers know.'

'Ah a fellow Mason. Well rather than call door to door, you should pop in at the Lodge tonight, Monday night is club night or whatever they call it, chances are my dad will be there if his hip is not playing up again.'

'Yes, great thank you. I couldn't get a response from the Lodge earlier so thought I would call round Donald's old address book.'

Back in my car, the relief of him being alive floods me, but I'm terrified of the realisation that if I want answers, I need to visit the Masonic Lodge.

The Masonic Lodge is an intimidating property in the centre of town but tucked away from the high street and surrounded by a brick wall perimeter. It has a classical façade and slate roof reflecting the adjacent streetlights. Five windows stare down at me, asymmetrically positioned, three on the left and two on the right of a big black door. A sixth, tall, round-headed window sits directly above the door, separated by the black masonic symbol of a square and compasses standing out against the white roughcast walls.

As I approach the door, I read a small royal blue plaque notifying that here once stood the Baysworth Theatre, constructed in 1887. I press the button, and the door opens immediately. An older gentleman stands before me, cropped white hair, glasses and clean-shaven. He is formally dressed, black suit, black tie, crisp white shirt, polished black shoes and wearing a small pin on his jacket, royal blue and gold colour. A sash of colour from his apron, fastened around his abdomen, sporting the same royal blue and gold velvet with the edges trimmed to give a circular line, with brass buttons scattered to look like stars against a night sky. His eyes scan my unease, and his raised eyebrows give way to wrinkles reaching to his hairline.

'Good evening, I was hoping to speak with one of your colleagues, Peter Mayne. I have just spoken with his son, who suggested I can find him here, it is rather urgent.' I say with false confidence, and purposely vague.

'Of course, please come in, we have finished our formalities for the evening and are enjoying tea and cake.'

The gentleman shows me into a narrow room that runs the length of the building with old wooden tables and chairs are laid out. A swarm of men are filtering out of the double doors connecting the main hall. They are of the same profile with an identical uniform to the gentleman that greeted me who is now accompanying me to a table in the darkened corner. He stops short and addresses the table, 'Peter, this gentleman was looking to talk with you.'

I appear from behind my host and hold out my hand to a much older man in a wheelchair with thinning hair, his wrinkles and folds in his skin so pronounced I do not recognise him from the pictures of years ago. I hold his hand rather than shake it, his rough skin so cold and bony.

'I don't have too many visitors, do I know you?'

'We have not met before, but we have a mutual acquaintance, Donald Lloyd, and I was hoping you could help me with something important.'

He innocently smiles and gives a nod of acceptance to my host who turns to leave. 'I will certainly try young man, but I have not been able to help anyone in twenty years.'

'I used to live in Baysworth but left when I was 14 to live with my mum, while my dad remained here until his passing last month. I was going through his paperwork when I found some old newspaper headlines about the local school facing a police investigation for sexual abuse by teachers.' Peter screws up his face, in deep thought rather than rejection. 'It was just over thirty years ago, you were the Detective Inspector on the case,' I offer, trying to help him pinpoint the time in his career. I pause again, not wanting to give too much away about my motivations for fear of distorting his response.

'I do remember, and I remember our friend Donald being at the centre of it all,' Peter replied.

My heart races and I curse myself for being so gullible. I slowly sit down next to Peter, bracing myself for what I want to hear, leaning forward.

'Can you tell me about his involvement?'

Peter scratches the back of his neck hard. All his focus suddenly on his itch. 'Peter, what was his involvement?'

'Well nothing really, some crank caller getting the press all hysterical about sexual abuse at Baysworth secondary school. We charged him for wasting Police time you know,' Peter said in a very matter of fact way.

'But you said Donald was at the centre of it?' I ask again, hoping for some more colour.

'Oh yes Donald, well the crank had a personal vendetta against Donald and made the serious allegations about him. Next day the crank confessed everything, said he was too drunk to think straight at the time but sobered up and confessed to making it all up.'

'Are you sure there was nothing else to it, I do know it was a long time ago.' I probe again, speaking slower, trying to draw him out.

Peter smiles back, 'Oh quite sure, I remember because they ordered me to cut my holiday short, I was in the South of France and was told about that a big serious investigation that was to start, no further details, no mention of the school. Barbara and I packed up the car and drove ten hours home thinking what it could be, a tinge of excitement if I am honest, only for everything to be sorted by the time we set foot back in Blighty.'

My shoulders drop, and I think back to the newspaper article wanting to test the credentials of his non-story. 'But, I thought you were the investigating officer?'

'Me? Oh no, I was on leave, as I said, I did not even know about the case until it was all over. In those days they always referenced the DI as leading the case when in reality it would have been a couple of Police Constables doing the donkey work.'

I feel like I owe him an explanation for my interest. 'Thank you, Mr Mayne, I read the paper and put two and two together, you see my brother was a pupil at the school and knew Donald Lloyd, we were his neighbours.'

Peter winces, 'Neighbour eh,' calculating something in his head, how to articulate something, it was his turn for a deep breath. 'It was the neighbour who was arrested for the crank call. Meaning it was your father that made these allegations, all because of some personal vendetta. He was very apologetic afterwards, but he caused a big commotion at the time I can tell you.'

I give a nod of understanding, signalling no further questions, the shame is written all over my face, the disappointment already eating me inside. Peter gives me a sympathetic look, searching for something to say as I stand to leave. 'I do hope Donald is OK, heard he had a fall after tackling a fire at his house, the poor bugger is in hospital.'

I bow my head and thank Peter for his time, walking away weaving through the gathering of grey hair, taking nothing else in as I leave and return to my car.

Donald's house is lit up with his usual array of lamps, but

I know they are timed only for show. I stand by my kettle watching it boil, playing back the conversation at the Lodge. I think about the vendetta my dad had and what could have driven it.

I need a distraction and check my emails. I notice amongst the Bitcoin opportunities, cash jackpots and B&Q reward points update, I have two emails from ACRO Criminal Records Office. I open up the first which starts with' Dear Mr Lloyd', it goes on to thank me for my inquiry and that I do not have any records stored on the Police National Computer or any convictions or formal cautions against my name. I open the second addressed to my dad. Typed out in big font are details of two formal cautions against his name reading; 11th December 1990 Caution against Mr Jenkins, 6 Hatch End, Baysworth. Section 5 of the Public Order Act 1986 for 'using threatening (or abusive) words or behaviour.' The second entry reads 24th July 1989 against Mr Jenkins, 6 Hatch End, Baysworth. Section 5 of the Criminal Law Act for 'causing wasteful employment of the police by knowingly making to any person a false report showing that a criminal offence has been committed.'

Two offences, serious in their own right, but it was still some relief to know it was nothing more serious, and not linked to the photographs that I found earlier.

I check my Facebook and read a message from Vicky saying how nice it was to meet up on Sunday and hoping I get some clarity or closure soon about Jimmy. Appreciating bell ringing might not be my thing, she also invites me to dinner on Thursday night. My smile quickly fades and my eyes drawn to a post from Caroline telling her thousands of friends that she is feeling shaken with an accompanying emoji. The bus she was travelling home from work crashed into a taxi and everybody was thrown to the ground. She only posted an hour ago but already has 89 likes and 34 comments. I start to write something but then delete it, we are still legally married, and I can do better than sending an emoji. I dial her number.

She answers on the first ring. 'Hey Caroline, just checking you were ok after the accident?'

'OMG, what are you stalking me now? You joined Facebook to stalk me,' she said, only half-joking.

'I've always been on Facebook, remember I poked you when I first signed up, and just recently I have been using it again to track down Jimmy's old school mates, but seriously are you OK?'

There is silence, her attention elsewhere, but then suddenly tunes back in, 'Oh yeah, fine thanks. It was nothing really, so how is it going playing Colombo down there?'

I used to love this about Caroline; she would lighten even the most serious of conversation, not in a condescending way but in a personal way, knowing my love of Colombo and my anxiety. I tell her everything about last night at Donald's and the shame I felt, I tell her about finding the photographs of my dad with some young children, needing her sympathy, wanting her attention.

'I cannot imagine what you are thinking right now Phil, but I can imagine how you will react, please remember you can respond without reacting.' I know what she means as I have heard it from her before. I want to please her, so I tell her about tracking down and talking to DI Peter Mayne to get the truth and seeking help, although that was a minimal fabrication, the assistance was not required.

'Ok good, good to at least speak to the police even if it was a policeman who retired 15 years ago. We chat for a few more minutes about the case, and I say goodbye. I can hear the hesitation creeping into her voice and then her deep breath.

'Look, Phil, there is no good time ever to have this chat but, the thing is, Harry and I are moving to the States, and I wanted you to know before reading something on Facebook.' Caroline pauses with an audible sigh of relief, waiting for me to respond. Too shocked to form any words I merely mutter the same goodbye as before and end the call.

Chapter Twenty-Three – 14 days after

I am OK with it. She's moved on. Moved on pretty fucking quick and now moving on to the other side of the world, but I am OK with it. I had some wobbles last night after our call, and between the first and second bottle of wine I wrote some text messages I now regret, and I unfriended her then requested her friendship again on Facebook. In a way, I feel the relief it has happened because now I don't have to worry about when it was going to happen. Our separation is permanent.

The alcohol caused me to pass out, but the call made me restless.

When I woke in the middle of the night, my mind instantly went to her, and in a trippy state flirting between wakefulness and sleep, dreaming and rigid consciousness, I replayed our relationship.

My mates and I were having our usual Saturday night banter in the Rose & Crown in Chichester; football and rating the girls from work. We belonged there in the dim light, sticky carpet and warm ale. Caroline stood out, radiating in a white Fruit of the Loom t-shirt half-tucked into stonewash jeans and blue converse boots. She sat opposite another girl at the corner table on low padded bar stools. Between them the tiny flicker of a flame casting dancing shadows on the scuffed walls like a magical carousel. Her fashionable round glasses providing the perfect frame for her piercing blue eyes fighting for attention against the reflecting glow of the candle. Her creamy smooth skin glowed through the cloud of smoke and dust bubbles, and I was encapsulated.

I wanted her to notice me. My mates continued like nothing was new, nothing was different like the most beautiful girl in the world was not sitting on the next table. Her golden honey-coloured hair swept behind her ears and tickling her neck.

I became very self-aware. The conversation on our table deteriorated to toilet discussions resulting from the previous night's curry. My cheeks burned with each stolen glance in her direction, catching a smile flashing across her face showing brilliant white teeth that dominated her faintly curved lips. I had worked myself up to a frenzy, and I felt uncomfortable. I was distracted, on edge, knowing the moment she would leave I would instantly regret not talking to her, it would stay with me as I slept, and it would be the first thought when waking. The only way I could relax and enjoy my Saturday night was to dismiss any possibility whatsoever of talking to her.

And then suddenly I was sitting at her table, being held prisoner by her intelligence and serenity. We talked, or I spoke, for what seemed like hours, the crowd around us a blur. Caroline was back in Chichester for a family birthday before returning to University in Manchester. She was studying Public Finance by accident after not getting sufficient grades for an Economics degree but had already emotionally committed to moving to Manchester. She ignored my joke about the cost of repairing potholes but did drop into conversation that she was single without me asking.

We went out every night that week until it was time to board her National Express bus back up north. She had a fantastic carefree attitude, an innocence that gave her freedom, but vulnerability too, I wanted to look after her.

Over the coming months we spoke a lot on the phone and met up sporadically, as the time and money equation was not complimenting my modest wage and, if I am honest, I did not enjoy her student culture. Despite all being from different parts of the country, her friends spoke with the same student accent at a higher than required volume. They also had a view on everything, and their opinion was black or white, but the real world is not like that, sometimes you have to operate in shades of grey. In the early days, I used to debate with them, but it grew tedious and pointless.

Caroline and I had fun when just the two of us, we were right for each other. I was her reality check, a link back to her old world or even the real world, to which she would soon have to return, and she really forced me to have fun, which I always did with her. By the time she graduated we had been seeing each other for almost two years, and although much of that time was long distance, it felt right.

Upon graduating, we planned on living together in Chichester with Caroline securing a job in Portsmouth, just half an hour commute. We were about to sign on a flat in the centre of town, close to my mum when Caroline dropped her bombshell. She had been offered another job. It was her dream job, a Planning Officer based in Glasgow. She did not even stop for breath after the word Glasgow like it was a minor detail, and it was clear she was accepting it. Our best-laid plans suddenly became an invitation to me which I could accept or decline, regardless the party would be going ahead.

Caroline loved corporate life and living in a big metropolis.

Her wardrobe changed instantly, and she looked terrific in her trademark pencil skirts and high heels. Her experience of living in Manchester made her better equipped than me in navigating the urban spread of buildings, the labyrinth of streets and alleys, and the pairing of poverty with affluence all under the same smog-filled sky. She made friends with ease, and we were always introduced as 'Caroline and her partner.'

If we were not out with her new friends, we were hosting her family. Her parents would stay weeks at a time, her sister and boyfriend the weekend, and her cousines for lunch or dinner. Her university friends would visit, the single friends dragging Caroline to clubs, my standing invitation only when couples visited.

We each brought our strengths to the relationship. I took care of the day to day running of the house and the necessary admin tasks. Caroline provided an outside-in perspective, arranging our social life, where to live, what to buy and where to buy it from, and in truth paid most of the mortgage. My facilities management salary from the council being forever subject to budget cuts.

Despite having some ups and downs in our relationship, we got married five years after arriving in Glasgow. Dad made his excuses not to attend, and I know my mum was relieved. I proposed on the banks of Loch Lomand surrounded by the most beautiful rolling hills and reflections on the loch and planned a romantic stay in an old converted boathouse. But Caroline was so keen to share our news that we instead dashed home to celebrate in the West End of Glasgow, champagne with her friends at a swanky club.

On our first anniversary, we began the journey of starting a family. It was to be a treacherous journey without destination, involving consultation after consultation, experimentation, strict diets, and ultimately a failing fertility treatment, and all the while costing us our savings. If felt like a vicious circle as the process caused us so much stress, which of course reduced our chances further, thus creating more pressure. The required changes needed to our lifestyle during this journey meant no more crazy nights out painting the town red.

We responded very differently to these stresses. I became even more withdrawn, and Caroline would later argue that I had become even bitterer. My shame returns as I think back to the bitterness I showed at the constant reminders of our failing. I would scoff in the direction of pregnant mothers in the supermarket, curse those parents shouting at misbehaving toddlers on the bus and rant at friends who had the nerve to moan about motherhood. I found Caroline wanted to talk about it, *all the time*, to anyone who would listen. She would be on the phone from the moment she got home from work until I went to bed. In contrast, I felt more comfortable avoiding the subject altogether, allowing it to bubble up inside, under the surface.

Our relationship prior was fun, full of the innocence of youth and hope. Our moods on nights out always seemed to sync perfectly. We could be immature and stupid together drinking shots, become all sociable conversing with strangers thanks to the champagne or become all philosophical and put the world to rights over a full-bodied claret. The common dominator to all this fun being alcohol of course. Even at home we would celebrate the end of the working week with gin and tonics or liven up those slow Sunday afternoons with a bottle of white wine. It got out of control, consciously having meal choices like hot chilli or a rogan josh that were best paired with wine rather than orange juice.

By extracting the alcohol, we also removed much of the fun we had in our relationship. In retrospect, maybe our entire relationship was based only on good times. A long-distance relationship, exploring a new city, and getting married brought out the best in us, as they might in any couple. The anguish of trying to get pregnant and dancing to the tune dictated by fertility treatment does not do that, it was the first bump in the road, and we crashed. Maybe it was the reality check we needed.

Towards the end, Caroline threw herself into her work, with long hours, plenty of trips away and began socialising more and more with work colleagues. I was jealous and resented this, as I had few friends, just work colleagues whose friendship ended at five pm each day. It transpired that I was right to be jealous. His name was Harry Herbert, her boss. She was sorry but not remorseful. Sorry for hurting me or maybe just sorry I found out, but not sorry it happened. After a couple of months of awkward silence and false affection, she moved out. We put our trendy flat up for sale, listing it as 'priced to sell' with 'no chain.' It smacked of a divorcing couple selling.

Caroline insisted on accepting the first low offer we received. The final nail followed only days afterwards when my boss called me into his office to inform me that the council wanted to make some changes. I have learnt when people say this, the changes are never to your advantage, and changes make life worse. I was made redundant with immediate effect.

I had no plan. I was packing boxes three months later when I got the call from Roger, to say my dad had passed away. That, at least, gave me a short term plan.

Chapter Twenty-Four – 14 days after

After a night of thinking about Caroline, much of my morning is consumed with thoughts of Donald. Peter did not mention how long he would be kept in hospital, and I have no insight into his health, but my need for some answers is insatiable. I need to know what he told the police after the fire. Not knowing feels like the start of my sentence. A million thoughts racing through my head ever since I jumped over his fence. I am meeting Marie from Camwell this morning, and then I will take a drive up to the hospital, I just wish my head would stop pounding so I can think straight for a minute.

As I close my front door, I bump into the builders from yesterday. I had forgotten about them. 'Hi mate, thank you for putting up the temporary door, I will call you when I have bought a new one and pay you next time, do you want me to make some tea before I go?'

'No need thanks, Donald's daughter phoned last night and left a key for us so we can crack on with the windows, she mentioned he is up at Rivers Hospital.' I never considered Rivers. It is an hour's drive, so it must be severe for them to bypass the local County Hospital.

I arrive at Costas and take a seat facing the door, the nagging doubt at the back of my head that she will not show after my garbled message. I tighten a napkin around my finger, wanting it to consume my attention away from wondering what truths she will tell me. After years of knowing nothing I am about to learn something of my dad and therefore my childhood too, was it all based on lies? At least I am easy to spot in Costas. I am surrounded by mums, legs shrink-wrapped in lycra with their designer prams, and teenagers in school uniform all on their phones getting the caffeine fix needed to see them through to lunch. I catch a glance of my reflection in the window, uneven stubble, bags under my eyes with a gaunt expression that I cannot shake.

I hold my coffee with both hands to hide my shaking and glance up to see Marie standing in front of me. She is no more than five feet tall, chubby cheeks, round glasses and hair tied in a bun to give her a few more inches of height.

'Good Morning Mr Jenkins.'

'Oh please call me Phil, nice to meet you Marie,' I say, realising I did not know her surname. After buying a latte she sits opposite me, wiping the clean table with a napkin then wiping her glasses with her handkerchief before poising them on the end of her nose. She leans in towards me, her thick glasses magnifying her eyes that fix on mine, ready to deliver my diagnosis. She stares at me hard. Is she sizing me up? Deciding what and how much to tell me? Can she hear my racing heartbeat? *Just spit it out.*

'I am very sorry to hear about your father. He was a well-liked man.' The relief floods my whole body, and I ease back into my chair.

'What is it exactly you would like to know?' she asks.

'Everything, I...' I catch myself, take a breath and glance to the door to relieve from her intense stare. My thoughts are a circus with a hungover ringleader. He was well-liked, I can relax, bite-size chunks of information.

'My dad and I, well we drifted apart over the years, can you first tell me why he was a regular visitor to the children's home?'

Marie sat up a little and leaned in a little closer. 'We don't advertise this much, but we advocate volunteering at the home, especially if they have life experience, much preferred over fancy qualifications I can tell you.' She pauses and allows herself a conspiratorial smile. 'The church introduced your father, along with Reg and Anna as part of some outreach program they were doing. We don't necessarily do these things by the book.' Another smile, more gratifying this time. She leans in closer still, I catch a scent of her rose perfume. 'Too much red tape and paperwork.' She whispers, inviting me even closer. 'Your dad and Anna were with us for quite a long period, and Reg is still going strong.'

I sit back in my chair, taking in a breath of air not consumed by rose perfume. I instantly replay her response, full of doubt, my dad was a regular at church and had valuable life experience. I play it safe with Marie. 'What particular life experience did he have to share?'

'Oh, plenty of experience that is relevant to the children of Camwell; depression, suicide, guilt, financial problems, custody battles, and yet despite all this despair he remained in a positive frame of mind and of course kept his faith.' Marie peels off her glasses to scrub them with her worn handkerchief, commanding her full attention. 'He was a real inspiration for the children who, in some shape or form, have experienced the same emotional trauma.'

I had no idea. I always thought my dad just disappeared into his shell, became a hermit with alcohol his only purpose. I also did not know about the custody battle, mum kept that very quiet. It was the term of guilt that unnerved me from Marie's roll call. Guilt from a heinous crime? Is that why he turned to the church, to repent? I sit forward on my chair, mirroring Marie.

'Marie, do you know where his feeling of guilt stemmed from?'

Marie takes a glance to her left and right, checking for prying eyes. She takes out her handkerchief once again and rubs the lens on her glasses as if wanting to re-focus. 'It stemmed from his debts,' she whispers. 'He did not go into any details of how he got himself into debt, but I know one of the consequences was having to cancel his son's place at the new school. It was some elite sporting school, with an elite price tag too. Your brother had passed the entrance exams no problem, but your parents could no longer afford it given the financial pressures they were under.' Marie sits back in her chair, holding her handkerchief tightly in her fist, inviting my response. I can't respond. My mind races to Jimmy being taunted at school, no longer big-headed, a new but same uniform having to be bought.

'Now don't be blaming your father,' Marie instructs reading my thoughts. 'He was unequivocal that Jimmy had been suffering for years with depression.'

Yes, but Marie did not know Jimmy. She did not realise how vulnerable he was. 'Did my dad ever tell you that Jimmy committed suicide dressed in his school uniform, on a day when there was no school?'

'Yes, he did tell me.' Her voice much softer now, the last traces of smile disappearing. She holds my hand between hers,

149

tilting her head. 'Your dad put two and two together, as I assume you did, sentencing him to a lifetime of guilt. I tried so hard to appease him telling him about the commonness of *dressing to die*. It's a textbook action in psychology literature, about the individual wanting a formality to the event. It's common for a suicide victim to be dressed in a uniform or suit, and I am assuming Jimmy did not have a suit. To me, it shows nothing more than the fact the suicide was premeditated.'

She was kind to my dad, but I know he would have taken the symbolism of Jimmy's old school uniform at face value, and I feel my first pang of guilt for him.

We talked a little more about some of the experiences of the children, some success stories and about those that were less fortunate. We finish our coffees, and I thank Marie for her time. As she walks towards the door, she suddenly stops and turns to me, 'If there is anything else I can help you with or help you make sense of, please don't hesitate to call. He did try his best you know, and was always well-intentioned.'

I stare down at my empty coffee cup, what else do I need to make sense of?

I saunter back to my car and type in Rivers Hospital to the map on my phone. It is a specialist cardiology hospital on the outskirts of Salisbury, and the journey is a pleasure to drive. The A354 is a picturesque road winding through Cranbourne Chase chalk plateau, an area of outstanding beauty. From the windy road, I can see for miles into the distance across a patchwork of fields separated only by the belt of hedges. The contrasting pastoral shades blend effortlessly with the dark green trees dotted like pillows of the land. The rock scree slopes of chalk providing the perfect canvass.

The beautiful countryside views can only hold my attention

for so long before my mind shifts to the conversation with Marie. I feel a sense of relief and pride that my dad rediscovered some purpose to his life. I also feel relief that his visits there seemed genuine, and a pang of guilt for contemplating otherwise. Nagging in my mind though, is how she made the point about not going through the usual channels which I assume to be CRB checks. I can only imagine his intentions were borne from guilt, stemming from either Jimmy or cutting me off or both. I feel a tinge of envy as green as the rivalling hedges outside my window that he afforded so much time to strangers when at the same time, he abandoned his son.

I know I am taking a risk by visiting Donald. I have no insight into his physical health or mental state, and I will be forever haunted by the confused look in his eyes as he looked up at me from the floor of his living room. That look of terror was all my doing, I was responsible for that. He would have been perplexed why I had set fire to his shed and so very nearly to his house. It is no wonder he swung at me, and I am grateful he didn't have a blunt instrument in his hand at the time. He had no idea about my vendetta, my agenda. For all he knew I was completely crazy. He would not have been wrong.

The tranquillity of the pastel green rolling hills is disturbed by the concrete car park of Rivers hospital with a rash of signage and duplicate warnings welcoming me as I drive in. The original hospital is a beautiful ivy crest, old building that now stands dwarfed behind the sprawling new structures resembling bricked portacabins. Grey faces hungrily smoke cigarettes standing outside of the industrial entrance doors, a constant reminder of the pain, grief, and desperation felt here. Shoved in front of the small reception desk are self-service terminals, two of the three with an out of order sign stuck across the screen.

An elderly lady sitting behind the reception desk wears two badges indicative of society today, one reads '*Here to Help*' the other '*Be Kind, I am a Volunteer.*' Signs litter her desk warning that aggressive behaviour will not be tolerated, another stating physical abuse will result in prosecution, and a third informing CCTV is in operation. Behind the elderly lady, is a spaghetti junction of directions, each colour coded by ward and department. Her nervous smile provides a crumb of normality to the desk as I ask for directions to where Donald Lloyd temporarily resides. After consulting with her file, she directs me towards Hascombe Rivers hospital, on the same grounds as the main hospital but a private wing and deserving of its own identity.

The hospital main entrance hall is a metropolis of retail outlets, stalls, vending machines and signage, with people wandering in all directions without destination. I follow as instructed the green signs, avoiding the blue, red, pink and white ones. The crowds begin to thin out and are replaced by abandoned wheelchairs and abandoned plastic chairs, the magnolia coloured walls bruised by scuff marks from trolleys. The smell of cleaning fluid is overpowering and warning posters on the wall unrelenting as I climb the wide staircase and cross over an internal bridge to double doors and a sign welcoming me to *Hascome Rivers Private Ward.*

The ward is deserving of its separate identity, a first-class upgrade on the economy version I have just navigated. Framed Art adorning the walls, real flowers in vases providing an aromatic scent, and literature showcased in oak bookcases with reading corners providing countryside views. Two nurses greet me at the reception, straight backs and hair tied back. Once again, I give the name Donald Lloyd as my purpose.

The young lady smiles and asks, 'Are you family?' She spots my hesitation straight away, 'Because we are outside of visiting hours, and it is family only.'

I take this as an invitation, 'Yes, I am his son.'

'Oh, how lovely in that case your sister is here too.'

I feel tested and call her bluff. 'Yes, a family visit to lift the old man's spirits.'

'Room 107 on the left-hand side.'

I sense her eyes watching me as I follow her directions. I was not ready to walk straight in. I planned to view him from afar, compose myself and approach him with my eyes open. I stand outside his private room, not knowing the scene that awaits me, with every move and delay being watched with interest by the nurse. I knock gently, and I am greeted by a female voice the other side, 'Please, come in.'

I open the door slowly, greeted by two faces looking up at me, the lady smiles, and Donald gives a nod, a perfunctory gesture.

'Oh, I am sorry Donald, I did not know you had company,' holding my hand up apologetically, inviting him to send me away.

The lady, middle-aged, dark brown hair and wearing a big woolly jumper, stands up. 'Oh, do not worry. I was about to leave.'

'This is my neighbour that I was telling you about,' Donald says without completing the introduction or looking in my direction. My eyes fall to the floor in embarrassment, fearful of the tales already told.

'Hello, I am Dorothy,' she says with a wave.

I return her smile out of relief. 'Hello, nice to meet you, please do not leave on my account though, I can come back later.'

She leans over the bed to Donald. 'Goodbye dad, you take care, and I will be back to pick you up tomorrow,' kissing him on the cheek as she leaves.

The air suddenly thickens as I walk to the chair that Dorothy had been sitting on and pull it back a metre away from the bed. Donald sits motionless, back rigid, holding his hands in front of him and already judging. I take a deep breath and meet his stare.

'Donald, I am so very sorry, I don't expect you to forgive me, what I did was unforgivable. I can sit here and tell you I was drunk, under stress and jumped to some very wrong conclusions, which are all true, but none justifying my actions.'

He sits up a little straighter in his bed, dressed in a thick blue dressing gown, clean-shaven and hair combed to the side, he looks surprisingly well. 'I don't know what happened Philip, and I have been sitting here in bed for the past few days racking my brain as to what possessed you to do such a thing. According to the doctors I blacked out and so was taken here, but I have a vague memory of your accusations.'

Please don't say it.

'Accusing me of killing your brother.'

I realise I have the indignation of having to repeat my accusations to Donald all over again, in the cold light of day, especially hard when I now believe it is not true. I need to buy some time. 'How are you feeling?'

'Oh I am fine, just been kept under observation for a few days given my medical history with my hypotension and finally getting a return from the insurance company premiums.'

'Good to hear, I am so relieved.' Any more small talk would be an insult. 'I owe you an explanation,' I blurt out, shifting my attention to the floor. 'I also owe you the truth as to how I reached these wrong conclusions, I am not proud of my actions, but I will be honest.'

I scan the room for a drink. Nothing is available. I swallow hard to rid my dry throat. 'You will recall, better than I Donald, that when we were growing up, Jimmy spent a lot of time with you and in your shed. He was fascinated by your war stories and developed an appreciation for the DIY you taught him. You were everything our father was not to Jimmy. You were well educated, had stories to tell, able to teach him new skills, had time for him, and most importantly, you did not put undue pressure on him.'

Donald allows a wry smile, a little pride perhaps?

'It is obvious now our dad was jealous and started openly resenting you and your relationship with Jimmy. I remember you two had a big falling out and at the time I thought it was over Jimmy, but mum suggested a misunderstanding over his rejection from the Masonic lodge. Somehow you were to blame. He built an image of you as being surrounded by secrecy and debauchery, someone who could not be trusted, which only intensified after Jimmy died. It was never discussed, but I remember being surprised you were not at the funeral. My dad, in his eulogy for Jimmy, did not even mention his passion for DIY or History, it was like he eradicated your influence.'

Donald gives a knowing nod of the head, a resigned look etching across his face.

'I did not give this too much further thought until I was sorting out my dad's financial affairs and going through his paperwork for probate. I found two newspaper headlines about the sex scandal at the school involving allegations made against the teachers.' I scratch my nose to disguise my pause, looking for a reaction that does not come. 'The date of the newspaper coincided with my 14th birthday, and I remember clearly how distracted my parents were during my party and how every parent kept speaking in hushed voices. I knew then something was seriously wrong at the time, and sorry it took 30 years to find out what.'

Donald sits motionless, staring deep into my eyes, consuming every word. I feel encouraged to continue.

'With this revelation, it dawned on me that I had always wanted to know. To understand why Jimmy did what he did, without any note, without any consideration for his family. Living with this huge void has been chipping away at me all my life without me knowing it, the itch I could not scratch. The mist was clearing, and I thought, at last, I was getting answers until I found out that the investigation was closed down before it even started. I was so frustrated, and then grew suspicious when I linked the investigating officer, DI Peter Mayne, with yourself. I thought of you as a suspect.'

The floor pulls my eyes down. 'You and DI Mayne were both Freemasons, so I grew more curious. I read up on all the scandals of links between the police and the importance of keeping brotherhood in the masons and how they operated sometimes above the law. I was angry. I wanted to take matters in my own hands. I wanted answers, and I am sorry, but I searched through your suitcase when you had it delivered at my house. I found your amyl nitrite hidden in your washbag, and I researched the place where you stayed with a reservation under a false name. Of course, your sexuality and your lifestyle is your own business, but I thought I found a motive.'

Donald's eyes widen and he reaches the palm of his hand towards me instructing me to stop. 'Enough Philip.' His voice stern, he is Mr Lloyd the headmaster all over again. 'You had no right going through my personal belongings.'

I look to the floor once again, 'I know Donald, I am sorry, I was so desperate for answers, your personal life is your personal life, and your lifestyle is your business only.'

'My lifestyle,' he chuckles only to himself. 'My trip to Romania was on official business through the Lodge. We have brotherhood partnerships with lodges in Ferentari in Romania, and lodges in Poland and Bulgaria. The local Lodge owns the hotel, and I was invited as their guest. They made the booking on my behalf under the name Almoner, as in *the Almoner*. That is my role at the Lodge, the Almoner, meaning the Caring Officer, responsible for the well-being of lodge members and their families. I was there to support a couple of brothers who have recently fallen on hard times and were in hospital. We had been fundraising for them.'

I open my mouth to apologise again, but he continues.

'Oh, and my little brown bottle of amyl nitrite was not hidden, I place it in the side pocket in case it were ever to leak. In a way, it is for my lifestyle, but not the way you think. A little unconventional, I know, but I suffer from hypotension, making me vulnerable to an extreme drop in blood pressure. It is linked to my autonomic nervous system that you might recognise as the fight or flight signal.'

My confused look encourages him to explain more.

'Depending on the situation, it sends the heart and other systems in the body signals to increase or decrease the blood flow. Mine does not. Therefore I am vulnerable to blackouts or fainting, just as I did after you attacked me. The amyl nitrite was merely a quick and temporary fix I needed as I did not have my medication, the liquid alert's me just as the strongest smelling salts would, to speed my heart rate.'

The guilt comes back to haunt me, cutting me deep this time, my acceptance of the pain a new experience. I no longer seek to dismiss it or to justify my actions as I have done thousands of times before. I see for the first time the tangible impact of my actions, of me drawing such quick conclusions, of violating his privacy. I played with fire, not by burning down his shed, but by hiding his medication.

'Donald, I am sorry once again. I did not have enough proof to confront you, yet with my warped sense of justice, I could not sit back and do nothing. I found the key to your house; I watched the builders replace it when they finished work one day. I entered your house.'

'You did what?'

'I wanted to punish you, hide some of your possessions, swap some artefacts in the house around to give you the impression you were getting confused. Saying this out loud now sounds so ridiculous, but I intended to attack your one potential weakness, your age, and therefore state of mind.

'Good God man, why would you do this?'

'I had been drinking and wanted to hide a couple of things I know you use every day, instant gratification such was my bitterness, your pills and your remote control, for example. I swear I did not plan this, I did not read the label or think about the consequences.'

Donald shakes his head slowly, the look of disappointment infectious. 'But why burn down my shed?' His voice bitter now, a creeping resentment sending my eyes to the floor once again.

'I saw the inside of your shed furnished like a teenage bedroom, my mind went straight to all those hours Jimmy spent there, and a blind rage just took over. There seemed no other explanation why a retired man would have video games, magazines and pop in the fridge.'

'You stupid fool.' Fire spreading across his face. 'You met my daughter Dorothy just now, but who you did not meet was Elizabeth, her daughter, my granddaughter, who is 14 years old and loves to play video games, read horsey magazines, and drinks pop. I watch her once a week while her mum works shifts in the hospital, sometimes she stays over. And like all teenagers, she appreciates her own space.'

I bring the palms of my hands to my face, partly to slap myself but mostly to hide my embarrassment. Already the word sorry feels meaningless and overused.

'I did not think. I lost all control. I wanted to be right, and I wanted an answer to the question I never asked. I wanted an ending. I wanted it to be you, and it was easier than the alternative. The alternative terrifies me. How can I live with myself, knowing that abuse was happening right under my nose? You told me that I never knew who my dad really was, I think I am finding out.'

It was Donald's turn to bring his hands to his face, rubbing his eyes intently as if changing focus.

'I am not condoning anything you have done to me over the past week Philip, and you could have killed me. But, hearing your internal pain has made me realise I could have been more open with you when we first met the day before your dad's funeral. The truth is, you and I have not seen each other for 30 years, and I had no idea that you knew so little. Your father and I did not speak, but I had assumed you and he did.'

'It is my turn, to be honest with you.'

Chapter Twenty-Five – 14 days after

It's my turn to sit up straighter and shuffle in my chair. Donald pauses for what seems an age, his look is pensive, and his eyes navigate the room, buying time before fixing back on mine, and taking a slow intake of breath.

'It is true, your dad and I had a falling out, a big one actually, which is also the reason I did not come to Jimmy's funeral.' A glance up to the ceiling as if recalling his silent prayer. 'He made it clear I was not welcome, but nothing to do with what you suggested. Yes, your father was a little sore about being rejected by the Lodge, but it had been me that put him forward in the first place.'

Donald reaches for the water at his bedside and takes a long, thoughtful drink, while I wait patiently for him to continue. Will he implicate my dad? Will I believe him?

'And yes, I did sense the creeping jealousy from your dad, but the truth is Jimmy and I enjoyed each other's company.' *I wince, did he see that?* 'In the early days, your dad was grateful as he knew little about DIY and it was not just war stories as you put it, Jimmy had a thirst for knowledge for all things History.'

Donald places his empty cup on his bedside, locking his hand together. 'It was your dad that made the allegation against the school, and against me, he lashed out. It was completely fabricated, he, rather like yourself, was driven by a vindictive motive, and when coupled with alcohol, it is a toxic mix. Brother Mayne, sorry Peter, had nothing to do with the investigation, in fact, we never spoke of it, not once.'

I remember the days of my dad and Donald being friends, long conversations over the fence, exchanging books. But something significant must have sparked his vendetta. 'So what happened Donald? I have seen the Police cautions against my dad for aggressive behaviour, going a step further than just a prank call.'

'If I am honest Philip, your father's gripe with me did originate from the Lodge.' *The Lodge, I knew it.* 'A brother from the Lodge in Bournemouth contacted us looking for help, sharing with us his grievances. His sister had been in a relationship with a man from Baysworth for several years and started a family with him in good faith. Instead of being there to support his new family, he spent more and more time away.'

Donald pauses, as if checking that I am taking all this in, I give the faintest of nods, willing him to continue, to get to the point.

'It turned out he had another family here in Baysworth and was using his job as a smokescreen to hide his double life. Our Lodge is *not* the mafia, and we were not going to threaten him or anything like that, his ask of us was only if we knew him.'

'*So what Donald?*'

'And could we have a quiet word, to remind him of his responsibilities and to find out his intentions.' *Of course, you scratch my back and I will scratch yours, that should be the freemasons motto.* 'You must remember this was the only way before the Internet. It was through connections that you found people in those days. That fell on me, both as the Almoner and, well as the neighbour to the man in question. I am sorry Philip.'

I sit frozen, ice sweeping up my spine, tasting the cold air getting sucked into my dry mouth, my eyes suddenly blinded by the light. I swallow hard, the air in the room suddenly thick. My mind races a million different thoughts crashing into one and other.

I always thought my dad was the loving husband, the loving father. My dad was always at home, except for cricket matches, visits to his sick auntie and working away most weeks. I shake my head to clear my thoughts. When I formulate this, and the reality that he was never the loving father nor husband, it becomes real. It makes sense. But how could he do that to us, how could he do that to mum?

'I can see you are shocked Philip, but until today, I thought you knew, it is why you and your mum moved away. I assumed it was discussed. I had a quiet word with your father, not out of spite, but I had a lot of respect for your mother, and I wanted to simply find out his intentions. He took this as a threat, and he thought I was emotionally blackmailing him. He went crazy, became very aggressive towards me, and started this big vendetta against the Lodge and me. He put a stop to Jimmy's visits and started spreading rumours, and when they largely fell on deaf ears, he started this witch hunt against me. It only paused when young Jimmy died, but then something sparked it up all over again years later culminating in the allegations against the school, picked up by the newspapers but thankfully instantly dismissed by the Police.'

I stare at the clock above Donald. It has a white face, black hands moving on each second of time with a ticking sound suddenly so loud it vibrates around the room, the numbers sit prominently in black font. I feel the anxiety building up inside me but hypnotically watch the hand complete a full minute providing a little escapism, feeling my heart slow in perfect tandem. I reluctantly drag my gaze back to Donald, his eyes search for mine.

'Are you ok Philip?'

I reply but only in my head, I cannot make my lips move as if I am underwater. The walls shimmering with the current. I respond only through my eyes, the rest of me paralysed. I fix my eyes back to the clock hands once again, the second hand approaching its vertical form, tick, he continues to stare at me, tick, a door opens, tick, some muffled talking, tick, the room brightens, tick, then my head bursts through the water to reach the surface, I can breathe again. A nurse is standing next to me, her hand on my shoulder.

'Would you like some tea?'

My focus returns, Donald staring at me, I feel the intense heat of his spotlight. I want to run but feel nothing in my legs. I turn once again to the nurse, 'Yes, yes, please, thank you.' I can't stop nodding.

I feel the air returning to my lungs and blood to my cheeks. 'I never knew.' My voice is broken. 'I never knew that is why my mum and I left. I had always assumed it was because of the strain caused by Jimmy.'

Wait. 'Jimmy, did he know? Is that why he.... You said to me in your house that I was too young to know Jimmy? What did you mean?'

Donald swallows a yawn, holding his teacup in one hand and saucer in the other.

'What does this have to do with Jimmy?' I ask again, impatiently.

He settles his teacup on his side table, his voice now much softer. 'Truth is I don't know, nobody knows. There is no conspiracy Philip. I was merely referring to his struggles, you were too young to understand this.' I blink the water out of my eyes. 'Jimmy had his problems well before your dad and I fell out over this other family business. Growing up, he was all or nothing, from one extreme of high energy and spirit bouncing at the door to someone who could not lift his stare from the floor. As he manoeuvred through his teenage years, he became more and more of the latter I am afraid. He lost interest in football, lost interest in friends, DIY, in school...'

'School.' I shout out. The term jolting my memory from talking to Vicky and the concessions Donald offered him that has been nagging at me. I take a steadying breath. 'What happened at school Donald?'

'At school, the teachers were all aware and we tried hard, carrot rather than stick approach, he was given the freedom to choose his agenda, in the hope he would come around. I tried hard with him. Your dad, he tried everything. He treated him with such compassion, took him to counselling when in those days it was only for the rich in London, and he got him medication, he gave up his job to take care of him, to sit with him each day and read to him. He tried hard to understand, but it is one of life's truism, that you never really know the landscape of someone's mind. He was fighting demons only he could see. As I said, there is no conspiracy. He found his peace through the only passage he thought available. The last flicker of light from his candle had gone out. When I heard those screams from your house, I knew, we all did.'

My head tries to make sense of everything I am hearing. Part of me wants to run out of the room, and part of me wants to stand up and fight him. How dare he accuse my dad fathering another child and Jimmy of giving up, neither are here to defend themselves. I stare again at the clock, expecting no answers.

The sobering silence sits uncomfortably between us. I search internally again. *I want him to be right.* I recognise my dad in everything he has said so far about seeking revenge, he would have felt threatened and would have chosen to fight back every time, especially if he also thought he had been wronged in some way. My dad's world was black or white, full of extremes, the spaghetti was the *best he had ever tasted*, and the man in the shop was the *rudest in the world.* He would have taken Donald's quiet word as an attack on him and our family, my dad's role as protector compromised.

With Jimmy too. My memories of holidays and playing football in the garden are mostly derived from photographs or stories my mum told me. My memories being her memories. Truth is I remember very little of us playing together apart from a couple of times in the garden and running the gauntlet of Donald's accusing stare to get our ball back. What I do remember is him locked in his room, the tantrums, being dragged to the table for dinner, and always being the primary concern to mum and dad. I recall again his argument with dad at the dinner table the time he wanted to give up football. It was not the first time, but they have morphed to one in my memory.

It is time for me to leave. I notice Donald is beginning to tire, his speech slurring, and the frequency of the medication being brought in by nurses is increasing. 'Thank you Donald, for sharing with me the past, and thank you for not pressing charges.'

I shake his hand, his surprisingly weak.

'See you back at Hatch End,' he replies. I notice for the first time his hollow eyes, displaying every one of his 75 years.

I sit in my car, hit by a wave of melancholy, and wanting to talk this through with someone who knows my history, that can me make sense of it all. My address book delivers a shortlist of one which I dismiss instantly. I drive home with the light fading, thinking what lengths my dad would have gone to protect his family. I know Donald did not tell me everything, he thought too carefully before he spoke, but I know it was severe enough to prompt a police caution for my dad's reaction. I stop at a red light on the edge of Baysworth and hear the rhythmic thunder sound of the church bells ringing, triggering me like an alarm clock the image of Vicky. I take a sharp left to drive up to the church.

The church looks different at night, less inviting with the darkness only sporadically interrupted by candles illuminating small patches of the stained glass. People are talking in their private huddles. I shy away from their glances and sit on a pew, tuning back into the chimes of the bells ringing. My trance is broken by footsteps echoing off the stone floor, and I open my eyes to see a dark shadow approaching me, blocking out the faint candlelight.

Only when he lowers himself to my eye level that his face lights up. 'Good evening Phil, lovely to see you, what brings you here?'

'Good evening Vicar, I was honestly just passing.'

The vicar sits next to me, his eyes matching his black cloak shining in the dim light. 'Have you been able to paint a picture of your father and find the clarity you were looking for?' He speaks so softly, so pronounced.

I smile, but only internally. 'I have been unearthing more

information and insights, although to be honest, the more I know, the less I know, I am not sure I will ever understand him.'

The vicar casts a rue smile. 'I know what you mean. Couples can be married and live together for fifty years and say the same thing about each other. Just be careful Phil, the character you will learn about is only through the eyes of others, and a good deed to one man can be an insult to another. I understand you did not have a chance to speak with Reg yet?'

Reg. 'Unfortunately not. I missed him at the Children's home, but I did speak with the coordinator there who I am certain only told me what I wanted to hear.'

The vicar clasps his hands together. 'I am not naïve Phil, I know when people talk to me about their problems, or when they have concerns for others, they often sugar-coat or exaggerate the facts to channel a response. But, following our chat after the funeral I have been asking after your father, he was respected. Determined to put right some of his previous wrongs maybe? Do not give up on him.'

We are suddenly ambushed by a gaggle of ladies wanting the vicar's attention, so I stand and head towards the door. The bells have silenced, and suddenly there is a hive of activity in the church with people buzzing about. From across the hall, my attention is drawn to a big wave towards me, half in greeting and half trying to get my attention.

Vicky walks over with her exaggerated smile. 'You came, oh how embarrassing, but what did you think?'

'Well I thought you were great, but a couple of the old boys over there were a little off-key at times.'

She giggles and playfully slaps my arm. 'So you are a bell ringing expert now. Listen, we usually all sit and have a cup of tea and a natter now, but do you fancy going to the pub for something a little stronger?'

We sit down in the old-fashioned country pub, no television, no music, no fruit machines. Upon her request, I tell Vicky everything that Donald has said to me from his hospital bed, grateful she did not ask why he was in hospital in the first place.

'So how do you feel about it?' She asks.

I think back over the day and the upheaval of emotions that it has brought. I don't know if I can put into words everything that I've felt today, but as Vicky continues to watch me in her encouraging way, I open my mouth and feel the words begin to tumble out. 'Exhausted. Guilty about digging up the past. But a sense of relief because as a family, we never talked.'

Vicky lays her hand on mine, the slightest touch to show her encouragement. 'When I was older and living with my mum, we never talked. And it has only been the last few weeks when I have been drip-fed these insights about Jimmy and my dad that I have realised how important it has always been to me. Until now, I always accepted my past for what it was, out of bounds, a closed book.'

'So digging up your past has been helpful, some clarity.'

'Now I know there was no blame for what Jimmy did and my dad passed away with dignity. Without facing up to this, I have longed for this reassurance, to rid my guilt. I have never been alone but have always been lonely. I have felt lonely with supposedly the people whom I should have loved more than anything else, my mum when growing up, my best mates and then latterly my wife. Caroline was an open book, her past, her memories, her feelings. I just could never relate to this. I always shied away from the past and avoided talking about my family or my childhood or my feelings.'

168

Vicky takes my hands in hers and tilts her head gently to one side. 'What you went through as a child was traumatic, something no child should ever have to experience, and on top of that your parents' divorce and moving to a new town, it shows real tenacity and resolve that you are not a total basket case Phil Jenkins.'

Like setting fire to my neighbours shed? I shake my head, willing the guilt to fall out.

'It is right to chase the past for answers. Unless you can connect to your true self, you cannot connect to anyone else.'

It was true that loneliness afforded me the time to grow, to build resilience, to create my own identity and strengthen my inner self. It served me well when we moved to Chichester when I dropped out of school and the move to Glasgow for a new job. I just had never considered its impact on those around me before. I internalise everything, my frustrations, my self-righteousness, my anger, until every so often it would explode, hurting those close to me the most.

'You're right Vicky. All through my life, I haven't wanted to talk about my past. I sometimes denied having a brother at all, it was just easier that way. And when I did, I painted him with one single brush—the boy who committed suicide. I was often asked why he did what he did. But I never knew, I thought no one knew. I always had my guard up, not wanting to discuss my feelings because I struggled to articulate them myself, I was hollow inside, my emptiness so consuming at times, and nobody knew how I felt. It is like I erased the whole episode, the lost years as Caroline once referred to them, but they extended way beyond my childhood. As Orwell said, *I wore a mask, and my face began to fit it.*'

'Hey, I love George Orwell. So you feel better?

169

'I feel different now, on the right path, a little more at ease. I have some answers now, I know Jimmy died without blame, but at the mercy of the most brutal silent killer there is, depression.'

Vicky smiles encouragingly to me, a flutter of her eyelashes, *was that intentional?*

'I know this may still be raw Phil, but how do you feel knowing you have a sibling, a family you have never met?' Vicky asks.

A sibling? For a split second, I had to join the dots to know what she was talking about. The mist had just begun to clear with Jimmy, and then this new grenade is launched towards me. I was so focused on Jimmy and my dad I had not considered the real tangible of the revelations from Donald.

'It feels so strange, like something you only see on television, the ultimate mystery to think there are people out there that are my family, I could be sitting next to them now and not know.'

We both turn to our left to see a bearded man, a little worse for wear, picking his nose and staring down at its contents on his finger. Vicky laughs, 'Let's hope not. It's probably a lot more common than you think, infidelity, DNA testing and Jeremy Kyle made it mainstream with trashy TV fame. So, what now Phil?'

I shake my head. 'I don't know. There is no instruction manual for this, I know nothing about them. First thing I guess is to find out who they are.'

We stand in the car park and confirm our plans to meet on Thursday for dinner, and I raise my hand to give a small wave goodbye just as she leans in to hug me. My hand sits stationary, cramped between us, hand resting on her shoulder and my elbow against her chest as she hugs me. As she pulls away, my hand remains frozen, making her smile at my awkwardness, my cheeks burning red.

170

Chapter Twenty-Six – 15 days after

Vicky and I are holding hands, walking through a dense forest, the twigs and leaves crunching under our feet, the branches of the tallest trees rhythmically swaying in the wind. Someone is hammering some wood, *bang bang*, louder the second time, *bang bang*. I sit up startled, transported from my dream to reality, and someone knocking at the front door.

I run down the stairs two at a time and reach for the door, only to be pushed back by the brightness filling the room. Roger stands in front of me with a concerned frown across his face.

'You said it was urgent.'

'Come in Roger, come in, when did you get back?'

'Just back now lad, drove through the night, it's the only way, takes half the time, and Mary sleeps so I can put on my Radio 5, now what is so urgent?'

I feel silly now I have some clarity, but I put the kettle on and sit down with Roger giving him some carefully edited highlights of the past two weeks.

Roger sips his steaming hot tea shaking his head. 'Poor Donald, he is a decent man is Donald. I tell you what Phil, you are a lot more like your father than you credit for, like father like son, flying off the handle as you did with him.'

Each time I tell the story, it sounds more and more ridiculous, yet at the time, with my tunnel vision, it made perfect sense. Vicky warned me last night that if you look hard enough for something that is what you will find. She was right.

'Roger, I spoke to Donald yesterday, and he told me everything he knew, but there are plenty of gaps. What can you tell me about this other family from Bournemouth?'

'Bloody hell Phil.' Roger rises to his feet, his eyes popping out of his head. 'You only learnt about them yesterday?' His wiry eyebrows standing to attention, his forehead folding in genuine shock.

'I thought you knew. I don't know why your dad continued to keep it such a secret over all that time. Cruel on you. I thought it would be disingenuous to talk about it at the funeral.' Roger looks up to the ceiling as if pulling the files from his memory bank, I long to fill the pause but bite my tongue.

'We only found out after you and your mum had left. I was sat here in this kitchen having a beer with him when he just broke down, told me everything. Plenty of tears shed I can tell you, and we hugged it out at the end. He was working in Bournemouth on a big contract, staying over during the week and in that time met some lass. She got pregnant. The silly old fool tried to balance both lives at first, having his cake and eating it, until things went downhill for Jimmy. That changed everything for him, all of his attention, all his energy went into trying to make him better.'

I stare at my dad's picture, Rogers's description of a silly old fool ringing true in my head.

'He gave up his job and gave up this other family at the same time. This other woman went crazy and used to bombard him with threatening calls, and all this time she had no idea he was already married with you two boys.' I shake my head, part disbelief, part shame all over again. How could he live such a lie, a lie to all of us? Were we not good enough for him?

'He had given her some story about him being a travelling salesman or something like that. Around the same time, Donald had a word with him, warning him for his own good that the net was closing in and that this other woman was associated with some unsavoury characters. And that's what happened. A couple of her family caught up with him, and he confessed everything, your dad receiving a couple of black eyes in the process and warned to stay away and to stay away for good. A legal battle ensued which he lost resulting in a formal stay away notice.'

Roger stares downwards, swirling the remains of his cup, looking reluctant to continue. I sit tight hungry for more, pointing my head towards him, encouraging him to continue.

'The guilt was too much for him and a year or so later he confessed everything to your mum.' Mum. Poor mum and her brave face, never letting anybody in, nobody allowed to notice.

'She waited until the end of the school term and then whisked you off to Chichester, and that's last time Mary or I saw her. We heard plenty about her though, from your old man. She gave your dad a tough time, not saying he didn't deserve it, but she banned him from contacting you while you were living with her, always threatening to tell you about his infidelity.'

I sit back and picture my mum. To the outside world, she was a sweet, quiet and unassuming lady, but I know if she ever felt wronged, she could turn in an instant, hell hath have no fury like a woman scorned and all that. She had this hold over my dad like no other, and I imagine him shrinking away rather than fighting her. I don't doubt her intentions were sound, but what about me? It was me that felt the pain of abandonment from my dad's silence. It was me that felt the self-pity and still do.

'Why didn't he fight her Roger, why didn't he fight my mum? Why didn't he fight for me?'

'It may be hard to understand son, but he loved you, and if you love someone, you love what is best for them and not what is best for you. Love sometimes means knowing when to let go.'

Roger slumps back into his chair, and a heavy weight lifted from his shoulders.

'So he let go, then what?'

'Your dad was a mess for years afterwards, and he knew you had been through so much, so chose to protect you by reluctantly respecting her wishes. He went downhill fast, never leaving the house, drinking too much, and became a real old grouch. If it hadn't been for what he'd gone through with Jimmy that could have been it for your dad. But he had seen the pain, knew the signs of what he was suffering from so the most important step he took was identifying that he had a problem.'

'How bad did it get?'

'I will spare you the details but it was tough. He only got back on his feet when he started opening up a bit and actively sought some help. He went to AA meetings and started going to church and doing some counselling, using his own life experience. He was starting to get back to his old self again when he tried to get to back in touch with his other kids, but their mother was still bitter and took out a subsequent restraining order against him. It broke him, Phil. He had lost Jimmy, he had lost you, and then he lost the twins, it was like life was holding him hostage.'

'Twins!' I leap to my feet. 'How old are they? Boys or Girls? Where do they live?'

I could have asked a hundred more questions, but Roger pre-empted with an aggressive shake of his head.

'I don't know too much about them apart from they are a few years younger than you, and their names are Robert and Rachel. I am sorry Phil, I do not know any more than that. As far as I know, he never attempted contact again after the restraining order, and he had lost again what spirit he found after Jimmy. He just plodded on with the church and with the counselling, but he was never the same. As I said to you at the funeral, it was the injustice that killed him. His intentions were always honourable, and of course he meant no harm to the kids, but their mum was punishing him for wronging her in the first place.'

I think of the restraining order, its formalness and coldness granted through legal courts. 'Roger, I have seen some paperwork relating to a legal case, and a big invoice that I think financially drowned him, but at least it proved he fought hard. I need to speak to the twins, and I need them to know that my dad tried, and how hard he tried to be a part of their life.' *I need to tell them about me.*

I open the door for Roger and give a firm handshake. 'Thanks for coming straight round Roger, I appreciate it. Although I am not sure your neighbour appreciated meeting me as I was putting the note through your door, gave me the fifth degree.'

'Terrible what happened to Polly, burgled twice, the most recent in broad daylight when she was in the back garden with her daughter, you just can't be too careful nowadays.'

That is terrible, no wonder she was so cold towards me. I wish I treated her with more resect now.

I text Vicky. I need to tell somebody. I sit down to think through what I can do to identify the twins, opening my laptop in the hope of some inspiration. My mobile rings, my screen displaying the caller name 'Vicky Facebook.'

'Twins!' she yells, mirroring my reaction only minutes earlier.

'Yea crazy. I also found out from Roger that it was my mum that forbid dad from contacting me as a punishment, and he always respected that until, well until it was too late. All these years, I have carried this ill-feeling against him because I thought he had abandoned me, but in his warped mind, he thought he was doing the right thing. When we did start talking again, the damage had already been done, our relationship beyond repair. The irony being history repeated itself with the twins. He was forbidden, formally this time, from contacting them. I need to track them down and explain. I know exactly how they must have felt for all these years.'

A pause on the end of the phone, and I imagine Vicky articulating something in her head, never wanting to say the wrong thing.

'You need to prepare yourself for something Phil. You had your dad for fourteen years of your life before the silence. You have no idea how much or how little he was there for the twins and what they can remember if anything. They may have been raised by someone else believing them to be their father or told their father passed away or was a murderer. Just be patient with them.'

'Of course, the way you describe those scenario's, it is like a soap opera.'

'I wonder if they are identical, I wonder if they look like you.'

The pictures, of course.

I run upstairs and pull out the photographs that were stashed in the garage and stare hard at the children I did not recognise with my dad. They do not look dissimilar, but I can tell them apart. Both have mopped blond hair and hazel eyes, but one has freckles and a fatter, rounder face with rose-tinted cheeks, the other higher cheekbones with a pointier nose.

'I have pictures of them Vicky, they are young, maybe four or five, but at least I have something to go on.'

'Cool. It's a start, and with technology these days you can get an image of what they may look like when they are older, the police use it to find missing persons, although an early teenage picture would be more reliable.'

A teenage picture.

A rush of adrenaline floods my body, and I run back downstairs to the dining room. 'Vicky.' I pause, catching my breath. 'I have that too, and I am looking at the picture now. Robert, Rachel and my dad on a walking trip.'

Chapter Twenty-Seven – 15 days after

I had assumed it was two boys pictured with my dad, but as I look closely I recognise the high cheekbones and pointed nose, and although the blonde hair is cut short, it's a girl.

They are aged maybe early teens, it must be Rachel. Robert, therefore, is standing on the other side of my dad, his head coming up to my dad's shoulder in height. His face has thinned out since the pictures of him as a toddler, but his rosy cheeks remain, his freckles fading and goofy smile now consumed by metal braces.

Moving from the back of my mind to the front is a tinge of jealousy. The picture I am holding in my hand, the image of his other family was the only one on show in the house, taking pride of place in the living room. It was his other children that he looked at every night having dinner, every time passing through to the kitchen. He was reminded of them every day with Jimmy and I resigned to a cardboard box. Out of sight, and stored in the garage for enough years for a carpet of dust to gather. Roger mentioned the twins were a couple of years younger than me so I would have been around 16 at the time of this picture. The age when I dropped out of school, feeling so lost and alone, the time when I needed him the most.

Our time together regardless of how infrequent and short

had been superseded by walking holidays with his other children. I inspect his face wanting a psychological insight. He looks proud, but no-one seems comfortable. His arms are outstretched behind the twins, trying to put an arm around their shoulders, but there is too much distance between them to look natural. Something doesn't look right. Dad had made an effort, dressed in the same walking clothes I borrowed to meet Vicky; the twins are dressed as if going to meet friends at the shopping centre on a Saturday afternoon. The picture does not look natural, maybe staged, and could be forced.

But dad was the same with us, forcing us to have family pictures regardless of the mood or what had just gone on. We could have had a big fight but then had to don our happy mask for a photo.

I think back to Roger, telling me how the custody battle was long and had killed my dad's spirit. That's what Marie must have been referring to when she talked about life experience. And all that while I thought it was for me. Did he fight so hard for me? I look at his eyes in the picture, feeling abandoned all over again.

I search through the papers again looking for any reference of my dad's legal dispute with the twin's mother. I do not understand how he can keep a receipt for a washing machine but not legal documentation, but I have learnt to look for what is not there with my dad. He was always a little dramatic, and I imagine him burning them in the garden to rid himself of his pain. Similarly, no papers are referencing his divorce from mum which I know exist as my mum had them strangely enclosed in her will for my perusal.

The will.

My dad would have referenced the twins in his will. I scramble to the kitchen where I scribbled down my dad's solicitor telephone number on an envelope and dial the number with my heart racing.

I tell Mr Pritcher a carefully edited version of my story and ask him if he has any contact details for the twins. On the other end of the phone, I hear papers shuffling for what seems an age before he replies. 'Mr Jenkins, what I can do is share with you a copy of the will, that is your legal right, as you are a named beneficiary and included are the other named beneficiaries. From memory, there are two other names complete with their contact details so we can send the necessary correspondence to them. I cannot put my hand on it at the moment and have a client coming in to see me in five minutes, so why don't you come down to the office and pick it up, faster than the post.'

I sit back down at the dining table and pick up the picture again. From nowhere, these two people have crashed into my life. They had my dad's full attention, and they had his fight. And now I will continue sharing my dad with them though his inheritance. I had not considered the consequences of splitting the inheritance with two other people. It would be a modest amount which I was prepared for, but I had not contemplated dividing this modest amount by three.

I cannot claim to have been the doting son who shared happy memories with his father or even cared for him in his later years. That was not me. But it was not the twins either. In Truth, none of us have a moral claim. My apologetic intention is born from my guilt of never really missing or needing my dad when I was a teenager. I had male influences growing up in Chichester, including friends, teachers and importantly Kenny.

I think back to Kenny with a fondness of our bond, I have never felt with my dad. My friends and I would often hang out at the sports pavilion which operated as an unofficial youth club. There were no formal open and closing hours, so I often stayed behind after my friends went home. Kenny was the building manager for the pavilion and other public buildings in the block. He was kind to me, often teaching me how to fix things. When he had a job to do, he would allow me to watch and take time to explain what he was doing. It got to the stage I would visit there to see if I could do some basic jobs regardless of my mates being there or not. Using Kenny's tools, I learned how to fix a leaking tap and change light fittings and door handles.

Kenny was a good man, always had time for me and could talk about anything. Sometimes football, sometimes politics, sometimes history. He was the only person that I felt comfortable with to talk about Jimmy. He once spoke about his own son being at University and having no interest in getting his hands dirty, he just wanted to make his millions on the stock market. Kenny knew his son looked down on him, a mere building manager. I could feel the distance between them whenever he spoke.

I did appreciate Kenny, and maybe it was because he was not my father and I was not his son, we could always be that little bit more honest with each other without being concerned about judgment. I ended up spending my 16th birthday with Kenny fixing a washing machine, when he found out it was my birthday, Kenny disappeared to his van and came back with a couple of Fosters. We clunked cans and sipped the beers while watching the first full cycle on our repaired washing machine.

I needed Kenny at that stage of my life, filling the gaping hole left by my dad. As I get into my car, I glance up to Donald's house and think back to Jimmy, needing what Kenny and I had—filling the void left by dad, those trips to Bournemouth.

I find the solicitors squeezed in-between a charity shop and coffee shop. A non-descript door opens to a flight of steep stairs with a threadbare blue carpet. I sit in the reception of the solicitor's office, which is furnished more like a doctor surgery than the high-powered lawyer offices in Manhattan I see on television. There are no floor to ceiling windows framing skyscrapers outside, or high-heeled receptionists in pencil skirts sitting behind a glass desk. Instead I am greeted by Elsie, dressed in an old green cardigan covering a floral blouse. I sit, as instructed, in a sagging green armchair staring at the tatty old Top Gear and Good Housekeeping magazines placed on the coffee table before me. The walls are adorned with posters and leaflets promoting legal services for accident claims and wills. I focus in on a poster promoting mediation for divorcing couples, and my mind wanders back to my reality, and Caroline.

The first time we spoke about our failing relationship, we talked about a trial separation, even making a joke out of the latest celebrity term 'conscious uncoupling.' I was still in denial and only now flirting with the anger stage, as I consciously plod through the change curve. The reality now being our trial is permanent, and we will be getting a divorce. In response to the poster on the wall, the financial implications I have not dared to consider. Our flat was not modest by any means, and it was in her name. The mortgage payments and utilities were coming from her account with my sole contribution being the weekly big shop and any essential purchases, the kind you do not keep receipts or a record of. My concern begins to flare just as the door to the office swings open and Stephen Pritcher walks to me with his hand reaching out.

Pritcher is wearing an old tweed blazer with green and brown tones, gold-rimmed glasses sitting on the end of his nose and curly grey hair. Rather than inviting me into his office, he simply hands me a sealed envelope, A4 in size. 'Here you go Phil, a copy of the late Mr Jenkins will and testimony, do let me know if you have any questions.'

I rip the envelope open wanting to digest it immediately, to check my understanding if necessary, while Pritcher is in front of me. My eyes are drawn to the three names and addresses listed under the term Beneficiaries. My name is top with an address I barely recognise listed beneath, our first address in Glasgow, and an address I have not lived at for ten years. My eyes are directed beneath to the second entry; Camwell Lodge, Children Home, Teyford, and the third; Mr Roger Knight, 2 Hatch End, Baysworth.

I turn the pages scanning for the names Rachel and Robert. 'But they are not mentioned Mr Pritcher, Rachel and Robert, there is no mention of them in the will.' His response is blank. 'We talked on the phone about me finding out about the twins, my dad's other family.' Saying this out loud in front of him leaves an unpleasant taste in my mouth.

Pritcher takes a step towards me and places his hand at the top of my arm. 'A will is a very private and emotionally driven instruction, often driven by motives at the time of construct. I cannot speculate as to why they were not included, but I do know it is not uncommon, that is why the contesting of a will is an industry all on its own.' It sounds like a speech he has delivered a hundred times before, to calm those left infuriated by the actions of the deceased with no questions ever answered.

'You should be relieved that the majority of your father's estate is attributed to you and you should re-read the letter to understand the claim of the Children's home and Mr Knight in the division of assets.'

I look down at the document but only to break eye contact from his formality. 'Mr Pritcher, I was hoping this would give me an introduction to the twins, but now I am back to square one.' I hear my voice, pleading with a hint of desperation.

Pritcher pulls over a chair and sits down, inviting me to do the same as I sink below his eye level. 'Phil, you should know that if there are indeed biological children of your late father still alive today, and they learn of your father's passing, they will have a genuine claim to contest the will for a fair share, meaning a potential legal case.'

I stand, frustrated by his rhetoric, so formal and robotic quoting legislation. I stuff the letter in my jacket pocket and stamp down the stairs, exiting back onto the street, slamming the door behind me.

I walk back along the high street, calming myself with a couple of deep breaths, gradually appreciating Pritcher for only doing his job of informing me, in black and white terms. Right now, my priority is not financial, but finding the twins and putting right what my dad could not.

I sit in my car, allowing my heartbeat to slow once again and pull out the document headlined 'Last Will and Testimony of Mr John Jenkins, 6 Hatch End, Baysworth.' I read that it was my dad's wishes for a financial gift of £10,000 to be made to Camwell Lodge, to be financed whichever way I see fit. Mr Knight is awarded possession of the lawnmower (or to keep possession, assuming he still has not returned it), and any left-over wine from the cellar of Mr Jenkins. I give a wry smile, relieved that at least my dad had a sense of humour when writing such a morbid document.

My image is disturbed by the beeps of my phone, and I open

the text message from Caroline, '*can we talk?*' With the phone in my hand, I scroll through my contacts and press the call sign next to Vicky's name.

'Hey, I know we only met up last night and have dinner plans tomorrow but are you free for lunch today? I am in town.'

'Hi Phil, sure that would be nice, you sound like you need it, see you in half an hour.'

I walk into the one authentic Italian restaurant in town and see Vicky already sitting at a table by the window with her big welcoming smile. Her hair is tucked behind her ears allowing her face to shine in the shimmering sunlight through the window. Her lilac dress fits naturally exposing her soft, ivory shoulders and lips carefully tinted red giving a smart appearance without any hardness.

'Well this beats my Boots meal deal, what brings you to town?' she asks.

I throw my jacket over my chair and take a seat, picking up the menu almost as a comfort blanket for my hands. 'I was going to suggest a lunch without boring you about my family drama.'

'Nonsense,' she replies, 'It is the only reason I agreed to meet. No really, it is important, and far more so than the tax returns I have just been calculating, so what's new?'

I pour myself water and lean in to avoid the prying attention of the next table. 'I went to the solicitor this morning to collect the will, but there was no mention of Robert and Rachel, meaning I still don't know their full names or have any contact details and I've run out of ideas on how to find them.'

Vicky sits back in her chair, with a sympathetic smile reflecting my disappointment. 'Did he not have some ideas for you? Surely solicitors often have to track people down.'

'I guess so, but then they usually have a little more to go on than a first name, in fact, he rightly dismissed all my ideas of contacting the births, deaths, and marriages departments as I don't have a birth date. He also advised against spending hours researching the archived court cases as it could have been conducted anywhere, at any time, and may not have even reached court. Needle in a haystack was his view, maybe he is right.'

My self-indulgence is disturbed by the waiter asking for our orders, and I see Vicky instantly perking up, affording him the same smile that she greeted me with. 'What is good here?' she asks.

The waiter takes his eyes off his notepad, and his face lights up, stepping onto his stage. With his rhythmic Italian accent, he preaches: 'You must have the mushroom risotto, it is made from the juiciest, tastiest mushroom, I know because my brother tells me they are the best and he is a good source of information, he knows the farmers, he knows where they are picked from, he knows where they are stored, he knows everything about them.'

'That's it!' I yell excitedly, much to the confusion of the waiter, 'I need to go back to the source of my information about the twins, to go back to Donald.'

The mushroom risotto is good and we make a point of appreciating their juiciness, offering our gratitude to the waiter. Vicky thanks me for the impromptu lunch with a kiss on my cheek. 'Hey, good luck with Donald, let me know won't you.' I skip back to the car eager to reach my own source of information.

As I pull into the driveway, I see Dorothy helping Donald out of the car. He does not stand as tall as he once did, so much time in a hospital bed at his age does this I suppose. I grab his small suitcase from the driveway and hover at his front door before Dorothy reappears looking flustered.

'Hi again, how is he doing?' I ask.

'Oh, he is OK, a little grumpy and the traffic was terrible. I'm going to be late picking up my daughter from school.'

I place his case inside the door. 'You go, and I will settle Donald in, no problem.'

Dorothy and Donald say their goodbyes with a promise of a call tonight and a visit tomorrow.

'Can I make you a tea or a coffee, Donald?'

Donald continues to his living room and sits in his armchair in front of the television, his head seeping back in slow motion into the cushion. 'Tea with a drop of milk, I suppose you know where everything is from your last uninvited visit!' He shouts through, to which I half-smirk, half-grimace.

As I hand Donald his tea, I look for a seat of my own, the only option being behind him tucked into the dining table, and so I kneel on the floor looking up at him as a child would awaiting a story. 'How are you feeling Donald?'

'Bored after being holed up in that hospital for so long. Now what's on your mind Philip, I can see you are itching to ask me something more than would I like a biscuit with my tea.'

I nod respecting his intuition. 'I have been thinking about what you said in the hospital yesterday, about this other family. I want to reach out to them and thought you might be able to share with me some more information about the freemason who contacted you in the first instance?'

Donald's face instantly screws up. 'Did you not find any paperwork in your dad's belongings? The legal strife was all he could talk about for years.' My mind goes back to my meeting with Marie and her parting words of offering to help me make sense of things. She also referenced that he was always well-intentioned. I imagine my dad being disturbed by the years of legal strife, and hurt by the supposed injustice.

'Never mind.' Donald brings me back to our conversation. 'Hand me that green file from my desk draw will you, assuming it's still in my draw and has not been re-housed to the freezer?'

I blush with embarrassment as I open the drawer to find the files covered in cornflakes that I had spilt over them only a few days before. *Why?* I sweep them away out of sight with my hand and pull out a green file, making a mental note to tidy them when I get a chance. Donald flicks over a couple of pages before handing me a yellow post-it note.

'Here you go. He stayed in touch with our Lodge for years after, contributed to our benefit evenings and we supported him when he was admitted into the care home a few years ago, I am not certain how coherent he will be these days.'

I look down at the scribbled note, '*Derek Chase, Jubilee House Care Home, Bournemouth.*'

'Thank you Donald. Did he ever talk about what happened with the family, the court case or events afterwards?'

Donald shakes his head, 'I never asked, and he never told.'

As I close the front door of Donald's house, I google the contact details on my phone and I hear the ringing tone before even reaching my door.

'Hi, I am an old family friend wanting to visit Derek as I am in the vicinity tomorrow, what might be an appropriate time to call in?'

'Anytime between 9 am and 7 pm is fine to visit,' the response well-rehearsed.

I pause for a second, torn between asking my next question

or not. 'And can you tell me how he is these days, I mean, is he coherent?'

A short pause, a telling sign the nurse wants to be diplomatic. 'He has good days and bad days.'

As I hang-up, I cross my fingers and hope tomorrow is a good day.

Chapter Twenty-Eight – 16 days after

I raid my kitchen for breakfast and cook a poached egg on toast with wholemeal bread. I notice a missed call from Caroline and press redial on my phone. 'Hi Caroline, sorry I missed your call last night, I was sleeping, how are you?'

'Oh dear, pass out in front of the telly after a bottle of scotch again?' Her question asked in her now familiar judgemental tone.

'No, just an early night, I have been busy sorting the house and all the administration for probate, what's up?'

There is a pause of apprehension. 'Well we didn't finish our last call on the best of terms, and I don't want us to fall out. I am in London for a few days. Maybe we can meet and talk about it?'

I shake my head and close my eyes, not really in the mood for one of her chats about feelings and relationships. And I no longer have to pretend. I stand straight. 'We are getting a divorce, you are moving to the other side of the world with another man, yes we probably have fallen out, and I don't see the need to meet up to confirm this. I feel good Caroline, and I am moving on.'

I surprise myself, three weeks ago I would have already been in the car driving to meet her, but today I am driving to Bournemouth and for the first time the present seems more important than the past.

I pull up at Jubilee House, a faceless modern building with flashes of white seagulls swooping from one concrete block to the next referencing my seaside location. I am greeted at the reception desk by the practised smile of a middle-aged woman in nurses' attire who, without needing to check, tells me room 17 for Derek.

The interior of the home is an institutional beige with an overpowering smell of cooking vegetables even though it is not yet 10 am. Cheap prints of yesteryear adorn the walls, a seaside pier, old cars, a dance hall, purposed to give a crumb of familiarity to those of a particular vintage. I knock on the open door of number 17, greeted by the back of a bald head poking out from a wheelchair.

'Hello, Derek.' No answer, not even a stir.

I take a couple of steps into the room and come parallel to the man in the wheelchair. 'Hello Derek,' I try again, crouching to his level. I shuffle forward a little more, to move into his eye line. He sits almost frozen in time, mouth open, and eyes without focus, pointed to the window. His face is devoid of colour and bony, years of alcohol abuse etched onto his cheeks and nose, impossible to miss. His mottled scalp is shining through a handful of unkempt long white hairs. I take his shaking hand in mine, slowly so as not to startle, feeling its coldness and fragility.

I sit still, transferring the warmth of my hand to his, repeating my greeting through a whisper. His mouth closes in slow motion, and I see his lips for the first time, the palest of pink colour shrivelled dry. His eyes meet my chest without recognition. 'Hello Derek, can you hear me?'

His look is one of resignation. As we sit face to face in silence, my eyes are drawn to the door to see a nurse staring down at her clipboard. 'Oh hello there, you friend of Mr Derek,' she says with an Eastern European accent.

'You will get little response from Mr Derek this morning unless you can talk about horse racing. He took medication one hour ago, should be brighter after lunch. You come back then and listen to him talk about horse racing.'

Before I can reply she turns on her heels and walks to the next room. Selfishly I want to wake him, give him a shake, brighten him up now so we can talk, then I can get home. For once, logic gets the better of my raw emotion and I head back to my car and take a drive to the seafront.

I park up next to a trailer swamped by a huge sign attached to its roof reading *'Andy's Snack Bar'* with a Union flag fluttering above in the sea breeze. As I approach, the man behind the raised counter greets me with a big smile, more fitting for a best mate in a pub than a total stranger on a deserted beachfront. His jet-black hair is receding, and darkened eyes dwarfed by his prominent rosy chubby cheeks.

'Hello mate, what will it be today?' He bellows with such familiarity I wonder for a second if he has me mixed up with someone else.

'Just a tea please, white, no sugar.'

He gives a nod of understanding. 'Take a seat, just boiling up the water and will shout when ready bud,' nodding again towards a couple of old plastic red chairs and a table, its legs chewed at the bottom.

I sit in peace listening to the waves crashing further out to sea, leaving only a soft foam sparkling in the sun. The sea is rhythmically running over the pebbles as it reaches the shore,

192

culminating in a sprinkling of spray skipping over them. I used to love coming to the beach during our holidays. After a long drive, it was always a long drive, Jimmy and I would let off our steam on the beach, tossing pebbles into the sea, skimming them against the surface, always in wonder at the disturbance a single pebble can cause.

Dad would spend hours with us searching the beach for the perfect pebble and perfect shell. Smooth and perfectly sym-metrical were my favourites, Jimmy would seek the shiniest and most exotic in colour. I would come home with pockets full, Jimmy with nothing, his standards not met. He would always hold out for something better than he already had.

We would take our nets for crabbing in the shallow puddles left by the tide, my dad always finding us a catch followed by intricate details about each tiny crustacean, which to us just looked like stones. He would tell us never to take anything at face value, always take a closer look.

Before charging back inside the house, we would be held at the door by dad. A brush down of sand from every crevice and a mumble about his precious cleaning bill: for holidays at least, he was always present, in the moment with us. I wonder if he did the same with Robert and Rachel?

The seat next to me scrapes along the concrete, and I look up to see the same man placing on the table two steaming hot teas in white polystyrene cups. He takes a seat next to me.

'My favourite time of year this, no crowds.'

I contemplate just for a second. 'But don't crowds mean more business for you?'

'Well yes, but I don't make too much from this, busy or not, I only do this to get me out of the house. I like a good natter with folk, and I would much rather have local folk, than a bunch of tourists asking me for a skinny soy latte and avocado sandwich. I mean I only have a kettle and basic grill for bacon or sausages. Nah, I prefer it quieter, read my paper and chat with the dog walkers.'

I chuckle inside, thinking that it's probably his wife that encourages him to do this, just to get him out of the house. I want to tell him we have never met, and while I am not on holiday, I am not local either, but before I can think how to phrase it without offending him, he continues with his ramblings.

'Not even my business, Andy is my old man.' Pointing up to over-sized sign. 'I promised him I would look after it, so the council don't move us on, just until he got better, and that was two and a half years ago. He is still alive today, but not going to get any better. I just don't have the heart to close it. He asks about the business every day like I'm running Starbucks here. The things we do for our parents, eh?'

I smile, to hide my shortcomings, unable to relate.

'I moved away straight after school, joined the army, and while I was in Cyprus my mum passed away, so my dad was on his own for years, so I suppose this is me making it up to him.'

He takes a big gulp of his tea and I take the opportunity to interrupt. 'Nice that you have the chance to do something for your dad, many don't have the opportunity or leave it too late,' I hold up my tea in a mock cheers way reserved for beers.

'You have to while you can. It must be horrible having regrets of things you didn't do or didn't say once they have passed away.'

My eyes fix on the crashing waves, his words repeating in my head, twisting my heart. I turn back but only see the empty chair, he is already back behind his counter, greeting another customer with a black labrador. That will keep him happy.

As I walk back into the reception of Jubilee House, the same lady sits behind the desk, her smile slips as she recognises me and her eyes are quickly drawn back to her keyboard. My walk down the corridor to number 17 is a stark contrast to earlier in the day. There is now a constant chatter and patients taking small steps in the hallway, most commanding the arm of a nurse or companion.

I am drawn to a commotion in one of the rooms as a man dressed in blue pyjamas is being restrained by two nurses. His protests are inaudible above the pleas of calm from the nurses. I slow my pace as I approach number 17 hearing a voice. I cautiously poke my head around the door, relieved to see Derek alone, commanding the same position as this morning.

I knock loudly to break his trance. I say hello again and approach him slowly, as you would a wounded animal,and lean down to his eye level affording him a full view of myself. This time his eyes widen and follow me as I pull over a chair. His fist bangs rhythmically against his knee.

I want his story, but know I first have to gain his trust.

'Hello Derek, my name is Phil, and I have come to visit you,' enunciating each word like a primary school teacher. It sounds so basic in my head, but my experience with mum has taught me to do exactly that and give time for him to digest my every word to piece them together, levelling the playing field as much as possible.

'Have you found my horse racing book and photographs, they took it you know?'

'Yes, I did,' is my confident, untrue reply, knowing it is also essential to agree regardless of how trivial or exuberant the statement so as not to cause distress.

I witnessed the pain that accompanies the constant state of confusion with my own mum's Alzheimer's, and the key stages that most patients move through. For my mum, it started with denial and her making great efforts to hide her memory loss, often choosing silence or elaborate excuses. She would often seek comfort for herself during this stress by whistling a familiar tune. For others, it might be tapping of a hand or even singing, some element of familiarity as a comfort blanket.

When her memory failed her regularly, she began to lose all sense of direction and would often be lost. She would lose perspective as she became unusually headstrong and stubborn, feeling bullied when I would not let her walk to town in the middle of the night. Her mind was more and more one dimensional without considering the reality, prompting the need for full-time care. It was like she was trapped in a phase of her life, the significance of which I would never know.

She kept asking for Eddie, who was her first boyfriend apparently and asking after her parents' dog, Cosmo. *'Had he been for a walk?'* This question was our standard greeting, posed to me twenty times a day, which is where I learned to reply *'Yes'* to all questions. Her accent was rougher, and vocabulary made up of slang I did not recognise, reflecting a much younger version of herself I presumed.

My mum was always a very calm woman, so it was disturbing to hear her swear in everyday conversation and at times become violent, the mind frustrated by the mist and choosing fight over flight. But even in those final days, there were glimpses of my old mum. A flickering of a candle as she recognised me and greeted me by name, before slipping back to her world once again. When she refused to eat, it was only a matter of time. It had been expected and was almost a relief in the end.

I was with her for the final months. That time being both a blessing and chore with excessive travel and time away from work. Dementia is a degenerative disease, forever progressive, and in my mum's case, she was unable to inhabit reality for long after it took hold.

Derek is bombarding me with questions that I barely understand and have no answers for except my robotic agreement. When he finally settles down and finds peace with my presence, I can begin.

'Derek, I am a friend of Donald Lloyd from the Freemasons in Baysworth, and I wanted to ask you something.'

He turned to me and looked me up and down all over again. 'I don't know a Donald.'

I take his hand in mine and soften my voice. 'You remember Donald, he helped you once, and you stayed friends, brother Donald Lloyd from Baysworth,' I see his mind calculating, reaching back into his memory bank and so I continue, 'He helped you find Robert and Rachel's dad.'

Derek nods jovially. 'Pete punched him, he shouldn't have punched him, Gloria didn't like him, so Pete punched him,' Derek shuffles in his chair as if re-enacting the event in his mind.

'Tell me about Gloria, is she Robert and Rachel's mum?'

Derek looks me straight in the eye for the first time. 'Gloria is my sister, the silly cow never visits, but Robbie does, Robbie is a good man. Pete punched him, Gloria's boyfriend, she had lots of boyfriends and lots of husbands. Pete punched him.' Derek holds up his wafer-thin arm and clenches his bony fingers together to make a half fist. He continues, only to mumble something about horses, slipping back into his world once again.

My eyes scan his room looking for family pictures, but there is nothing personal on show, no photographs, no cards, and no pictures. His one shelf under his side table is empty, and a wardrobe full of old clothes squeezed into each shelf. I lean in towards Derek once again to bring him back, but I know it is futile, his eyes are fixed on the arm of his wheelchair and he mumbles to himself about horses again nodding his head frantically.

As I walk out of the room, I catch sight of the nurse from this morning. 'Hi, I was wondering, do you know Robbie who visits Derek from time to time?'

'I don't know him,' she replies without breaking stride. I ask the same question to another nurse, who was earlier restraining the man in the blue pyjamas, but get the same response. As I head towards the exit, I play in my head how to ask the receptionist without being dismissed quite so easily. As I turn the corner, I see the desk unattended and clear except for a visitor book.

I flick back through the pages searching for names of Derek's visitors but find nothing. I start again, flicking through slower this time, and see an entry under *Mr D. Chase* from a month ago by '*RE*,' time in 12.33 and time out 15.38 with a car registration of BL26 8QP. It is the only entry in the book to visit Derek, although I have mixed feelings if this is one of the twins. Doubt stemming from the formal name afforded to their uncle written in the visitor book. But three hours spent with Derek suggests a family member rather than social worker.

Sitting in my car, I google the number plate without success. I think of contacting the DVLA who would have the owner details, but why would they give it to some random guy contacting them? I scroll through the contacts on my phone, looking for inspiration from the names that may be able to help. I pause at the one number on my phone, which has all the connections. A flash of adrenaline shoots through my body, the growing excitement that I am getting closer.

Chapter Twenty-Nine – 16 days after

'Hello, Donald.' I stand smiling, but my greeting is returned with an eye roll and a shrug of the shoulders. 'Did you not hear the bell the first time?' I cheekily ask.

'I have just seen off Dorothy and all the fussing that comes with her, you can come in for five minutes.' Donald walks ahead and into the living room taking a seat at the dining table, which I accept as a good sign, inviting me to also sit down rather than kneeling at his feet as before.

'Donald, I need to apologise.'

His arms fold with purpose, bracing himself. 'Bloody hell Philip, now what have you done?'

I make a point of looking him straight in the eye. 'This time, I need to apologise on behalf of my dad. I know you had your differences, but what he did was inexcusable'. I reach into my pocket and pull out the thin, tattered envelope, setting it down on the table in front of him.

Donald reaches for his glasses and bends over the table, inspecting the envelope, before pulling out the medal. 'Well, well, this is very interesting, you have Pip,' he holds the medal between his thumb and forefinger, turning it over and brushing his thumb over it, releasing a smirk of satisfaction and a knowing nod. 'And what would you like me to do with this?' His eyes strain above his reading glasses to meet mine, throwing me off-guard.

'I am returning it to you. I found it in an old box of my dad's possessions hidden in the garage, I assumed it was yours, but who is Pip?'

Donald gave the medal a second look, turning it over in his fingers.

'Pip is the campaigning medal from WW1. The 1914 Star was always awarded with Squeak and Wilfred, more formally known as the British War medal and the Victory medal. But this is not mine you understand, and this is an original. You see here, the recipient's number, rank, and regiment stamped on the back in block capitals.' I lean in closer to look again at what I have already read.

'So my dad did not steal it from you?' I hear the respite in my voice. 'It is just I noticed the empty mount in your draw, and I assumed you were missing a medal, and then I put two and two together.'

'Jumping to conclusions again Philip? He did not steal it from anyone. This was his father's. He was proud of your Grandad, but at the same time, he felt resentment about being left so young without a father himself and his mum without a husband. He never really liked to talk about the war, which is why he got upset with me for encouraging Jimmy.'

My eyes find the framed medals on Donald's wall next to paintings of tanks and RAF planes. Reading my thoughts, he interjects. 'I have only ever been a keen reader, observing from a distance. Neither I nor any of my family has ever even held a gun let alone gone into battle.' His look is one of resignation. 'My father ran a newsagents in Guildford.'

'But I thought...'

'You and Jimmy both did, your father too, and others no doubt. I never lied to anybody, people just assumed, and the persona fitted rather well with my career as a History teacher. My passion and interest in the Great Wars are genuine, sadly the memorabilia on my wall is not.'

The silence stretches out in the space between us, our eyes both fixed on the table.

'You are right. It was our mistake.' I need to say something, anything. 'Is there anything I can do for you, anything at all?'

Donald returns a rare smile. 'You can do the one thing Dorothy refuses.'

I raise my eyebrows with apprehension.

'You can fix me a bloody drink.'

My confidence returning, I pour Donald a whiskey with lemonade and ice, and myself a cup of tea.

Donald offers me the invitation I was hoping for while rotating his whiskey glass. 'Did you investigate the name I gave you in Bournemouth?'

I take a second not to seem too eager. 'I met him this morning actually, and he was a little confused, dementia most probably. I did ascertain some information, although I may need some help from someone with connections in the police force.'

'Well spit it out chap, was it a tattoo, a criminal record, what was it?'

'A car license plate from the visitor log, no name, but initials that fit one of the twins and an admission from Derek that Robbie visits regularly. However, he was very confident for someone so confused, too confident maybe. I just need to trace the owner of the registration plate, and I have found him.'

'Twins, wow I never knew it was twins.' Donald sits back in his chair with a wry smile, no doubt thinking of my dad and the predicament he was in. 'Well, good luck son, you deserve to know.' I sit quietly and wait for more, for him to take my bait.

'Thanks Donald, and I know I do not deserve your help after everything I have done. Still, I was hoping you could maybe call upon some old buddies from the force or maybe some old brothers that have connections to the force. I have no-one else to ask.'

Donald folds his arms again and leans back in his chair, shutting one eye. 'My connections and brothers are the same people, the problem being they either make Derek look like a spring chicken or are six feet under already. I mean you met Peter Mayne, they pump him full of drugs and let him out for two hours a week to join our social meet up.'

He had a point, from my brief liaison with the Lodge, most looked like their best years were undoubtedly behind them.

'Leave it with me Philip, and I will see what I can do, no promises though.'

I write down the registration number on his pad. 'Thanks Donald, now why don't you grab the newspaper and your drink, and I will run around the house with the Hoover and duster to keep Dorothy happy.'

I put right all the chaos I remember setting off in the house, returning pictures, cleaning cereal out of drawers, replacing lightbulbs. I quickly lose track of time and shout a goodbye as I leave through the door and go straight to my car.

It suddenly dawns on me what I am doing and where I am going. Meeting Vicky on the moors was casual, and the drinks after church and lunch were very much spur of the moment. Dinner tonight is our first real date. My mind inexplicitly wanders back to the image of Caroline packing up her boxes, and I realise I'm no longer paralysed with the fear of having to date again. I allow myself a smirk in the mirror, testament to Vicky more than my personal growth, that I only feel excited and not gut-wrenching nerves. She has a very natural disposition and puts me at ease, and I remind myself there and then not to take advantage of this in the future. Showering and clean clothes being a basic requirement next time.

I jog through the High Street, quickly realising how unfit I have become. 'Sorry I am a few minutes late Vicky,' I say holding up the palms of my hands. 'You won't believe me, but I was cleaning Donald's house.'

'Well if you are trying to impress me it is working.'

We talk for hours, about Vicky's career plans, her faith, her love of amateur theatre and of course a little of my day with Derek and Donald. We are the last ones to leave the restaurant, and I had not even noticed the tables around us emptying. Without pause or too much thought, we kiss goodnight, her mouth fitting perfectly against mine.

As I settle on the sofa to watch the late edition of the news on television, I receive a text message from Vicky. '*I had a lovely time tonight Phil x*' I smile and immediately reply '*me too x*' before turning off the grim reality of wars and famines and go to bed. Today has been a good day.

Chapter Thirty – 17 days after

I wake to the song of the nightingale from my garden and open my eyes to an orange glow around my curtains, signalling the early morning sun. I open the curtains, the dew in the garden glistens, blurring the dark green of the grass beneath. I slip on my dad's brown walking boots and his bright red waterproof jacket, grab a cereal bar from the kitchen and head out of the house, turning right at the end of the driveway and walk the ten metres to the sty, signalling the start of the Baysworth woods.

The woods are never silent, the crunch of the brown stiffened leaves and twigs underfoot, birds crying out in song, and always an animal scurrying somewhere leaving a domino effect of rustling bushes. Above me, the leaves flutter and dance to their own tune, a moving ceiling.

The first memory that comes flooding back is how much cooler the woods always were under the shade of the feathery leaves, mum never letting us leave without our big coat. My dad was no rambler, but when he walked through these same woods, his head would be fixed upwards, hypnotised by the beautiful swaying branches and on the lookout for woodpeckers. Jimmy and I would be racing ahead trying to catch sight of a rabbit or fox, prodding our sticks in each burrow.

I clamber up the hill, affording myself a rest at its peak to drink in the views and devour my cereal bar. I am taken aback by the expanding landscape of greenery. I compare it to the grey tower blocks that would consume the same viewpoint in any city with factory smoke billowing out, and of course the familiar traffic hum, which you can never really escape. I feel grateful to have this on my doorstop..

My descent is a leisurely one, and I feel invigorated as I return to the house, stamping my feet on the driveway to rid the excess mud.

'You are up with the birds this morning,' a now-familiar voice shouts from behind me. I turn to see Donald striding towards me, holding up a post-it note as it if were the Olympic torch.

'Just earning my breakfast, Donald,' I reply before my attention turns to his offering held at my eye-level.

'Don't ask and don't tell is our motto on passing information, please respect that, oh and enjoy your breakfast.'

I shake his hand warmly. 'Thank you Donald. This means a lot to me.'

I stand anchored to the spot as I read Donald's scribble, *'Rachel Evans, last registered address. 24 Cannon Street, Poole, Dorset BH11 1TH'*. It must be her. I spring my laptop open, tapping ferociously at the table as it takes an age to power up. I google 'Rachel Evans, Poole' returning only a handful of articles about a teenage gymnast who is representing GB at the next Olympics. I search using Facebook, and amongst the hundreds of Rachel Evans, two have their hometown listed as Poole.

One is an elderly lady, the other shows only a cat as the profile picture and little else once I click on the profile. I search the address and find images on Streetview of the house, a typical

Victorian seaside town property, semi-detached, painted white stone wash. I zoom in closer to spot any clues from the windows of its inhabitants, but see only stickers on the small upstairs window, a children's room perhaps?

I open another tab on the search engine, promising myself to return to search in more depth. This time I search 'Robert Evans Poole.' I read each entry carefully, clicking on the ambiguous ones but turning up no concrete leads. As I reach page eighteen of ninety-six, I shut it down with the dawning reality that the surname Evans could be exclusively for his sister taken after marriage and Robbie could be living anywhere in the world.

I phone Vicky. 'Hey, quick poll, if you had a long lost brother who you had never met, maybe not even known about would you a) want him to phone or b) want to meet him face to face first?' I follow up with the annoying sound of the countdown clock speeding her response.

'Oh crikey, if I knew about him then face to face, if I didn't know about him it would be by telephone, give me time to get my head around the fact I have a brother first, meet him second. Is that the right answer, do I get a prize?'

I laugh out loud. 'Only time will tell Vicky, I have an address, and in response to your scenario, truth is I don't know if dad ever mentioned me, and if he did, they never found me.'

'Stop with the self-pity Jenkins, they never found your dad either, and he didn't move to Scotland. Please remember to at least consider though, that there is a possibility that they knew, but chose not to act for whatever reason, as we talked about on the phone a couple of days ago.'

I pause for a second. 'You are right of course, but of all the uncertainties and moving parts I have to deal with, I have selfishly put this scenario at the bottom of the pile, a problem

for future Phil,' I joke without response. The doorbell rings
and I say my goodbyes to Vicky as I open the door to Roger.

He stands in front of me, hands-on-hips, pushing his belly
out with his arched back, whitening hair firing in every direction, looking more and more like a retired farmer as each day
passes.

'Now then lad, I have come for my vintage champagne and
fine wine. Where is that secret door to the cellar?'

'So, you received a copy of the will.'

'I did, the cheeky sod, I will be lucky to find a tin of stout left
in the house. No mention of the twins I see.'

I move aside inviting Roger into the house, and he walks
straight to the dining room table, picking up the photograph
on the table of dad, Robbie and Rachel in their walking gear. 'Is
this them?'

'Yes, at least I am ninety-nine per-cent sure it is. I have
Rachel's address and was just contemplating my next move,
which depends on if they knew about me or not. You can see
in the photo that they are old enough to ask questions about
his past, and present. My dad and I were not close, but surely,
he would not have dismissed my very existence. But then, I ask
myself, why didn't they come looking for me?'

Roger pulls out a chair and sits down, elbows on the table
propping up his head between his hands. 'The thing you have
to remember is that the legal matter and its outcome broke
your dad, as I said before. He slipped into a terrible depression
and did not talk to anyone for years. He cut himself off from
the world. Even if they did make contact, there is no guarantee
he would have returned it, and you know more than anyone
how it feels to be abandoned by your dad.'

He turns his head to me. 'Also Phil, if it was more recently that they reached out then again there's little chance they had a response, the cancer consumed him.'

'How was he towards the end Roger?'

Roger blows the air from his cheeks. 'The thing about cancer is that it can always exceed your expectations. In his final days, he was pumped full of so much morphine his whole complexion changed. Even with an oxygen mask, you could hear the strain on his lungs. When the fog in his eyes cleared, all I could see was regret and fear, it can always exceed your darkest moments. I am sorry son.'

My whole body floods with regret. I think of the sacrifices he made in staying away, thinking he was doing the right thing. I think back to my unanswered letters and the hours of contemplation in my bedroom as a teenager.

'Maybe the only difference between the twins and I is that I got a second chance after mum died, which I wasted, it was too late. I cannot let his suffering be in vain.' I grab my car keys and head to the car, tapping the postcode into google maps without breaking stride.

The first realisation of what I am doing and its magnitude hits me just fifteen minutes into my journey. My stomach turns, hands clasping tighter to the steering wheel, and I feel my shirt clinging to my back. I turn on the radio wanting a distraction but grow quickly irritated by the adverts and mute it. I try and control my mind, I think of Vicky, but only images of Rachel appear, and what am I supposed to say. I run through a script in my head, on a continuous loop, each time it becomes more detailed, more like a role play. I begin to feel more secure as I envisage our conversation, my breathing slowly returning to normal when suddenly my confidence shatters again. I realise I have left the photograph of Rachel, Robbie, and dad on the dining room table.

Every conversation I have been envisaging has the photograph as an integral prop. I am also thirsty. I don't have a jacket either, what if Rachel suggests going for a walk?

I pull the steering sharply left to pull into a lay-by. I turn off my engine leaving only the hum of the traffic from beyond the window. I think about turning around, abandoning until tomorrow. She is not expecting me so she would be none the wiser of my cowardly action. More self-doubt steamrolls into my mind; she may be on holiday, is it school half-term? She might not even live there; it took months of Caroline nagging me before I informed the DVLA we had moved.

I wish I was sitting in my living room right now, sipping a beer and watching television, not a care in the world. But staring down at me in the room would be the picture of dad and the twins. Mocking me. I want answers to his trial, for that is what this is now. I need to know why he continued to keep this secret from me for all these years, they are my family too, yet he did his best rob me of this.

I put my foot down on the accelerator to send a signal of purpose to my mind.

I turn into Cannon Street, my mind switching to practicalities. Warning signs every ten metres tell me the street is for residents only with a permit required. My anxiety increases as I debate the merits of parking further away, concluding the walk is a chance to clear my mind. I drive slowly past number 24 like seeing a celebrity in the flesh for the first time, it is familiar to me, yet I have never seen it with my own eyes. I turn left out of Cannon street and ignore the next two streets running parallel, assuming them to be the same. I approach a small row of shops and slow down to read the parking sign allowing two hours maximum with no return allowed. As I park up, it dawns on me that I should come bearing gifts, or in this case, flowers from the florist, having little faith in the butchers, the charity shop or the newsagents that complete the row of local shops.

A bell rings announcing my arrival, and a young girl leaves her colleague in the back room to take up a position behind a counter. She greets me with a smile while also assessing the level of assistance I need as I stand in the shop and spin slowly 360 degrees looking for inspiration, finding the choice somewhat overwhelming.

She leaves the safety net of her counter and approaches me slowly, her olive skin colour complimented by long wavy dark hair.

'Girlfriend, wife, mother or work colleague?' She asks with an enthusiastic smile, which I return with silence as I run through the list again in my head.

'Err none of those,' I finally reply.

'What is her style?'

I shrug my shoulders.

'Her taste?'

I shrug my shoulders again and look to the floor, sure that my guilt is fuelling her suspicion further.

'OK, what is the occasion, sympathy, apology or I have a secret crush on you for years and I want you?' Her tone suddenly flirtatious. The girl reads the horror in my face. 'Oh sorry, I did not mean to offend you, my boss is on the phone out the back, let me leave you alone to browse, and she will be right out to help to you.'

I don't need to say anything, but it is rare to meet a shop assistant with a sense of humour and a smile, so I feel obliged to say something to defend my awkwardness.

'I am sorry, I just was not prepared for the questions, truth is I am about to meet my sister for the first time, so I am a little nervous and a little vague when it comes to knowing her favourite flower.' I surprise myself with my open confession to a complete stranger.

The assistant's eyes light up. 'Oh, how exciting for you both, no more questions from me, I suggest tulips, everybody likes tulips, and they don't sell these at the petrol station so she will recognise the effort, I will wrap them up for you.'

I get little change from £30, but then the guy she describes buying flowers from the petrol station is me, or sometimes the supermarket if it has a reduced yellow sticker on it. I thank the assistant for all her help, and as I trigger the bell for a second time opening the door, she shouts after me, 'I hope it works out, good luck with everything.'

He parting wishes stay with me as I walk to the house, unsure if she is referring to meeting Rachel or the rest of my life. Maybe they are intertwined, as if my life is about to be mapped out in the next hour.

I check my watch for the fourth time, yet I can be neither early nor late. I study each house number as I pass, yet I already see my destination. I walk past number 26 in slow motion and come face to face with the red door of number 24. My heart beats faster, and I feel my grip tightening on the plastic wrapping around the stems, noticing for the first time the spicy aromatic smell of the tulips. I take a deep breath and knock loudly. I hear the approaching footsteps from shoes on a wooden floor, in perfect tandem with my beating heart, a twist of the lock and the door opens.

Chapter Thirty-One

'Hi Rachel Evans,' I say, sounding like I am half-questioning, half-making a statement.

'Yes.'

My eyes are drawn to her high cheekbones straight from photographs, and her wavy blonde hair. She has deep-set hazel eyes and a warming smile dominating her face. She moves an inch to her left blocking out the sunlight from the window behind her and morphing into a silhouette showing her tall slim body and frills from her floral dress. I feel the cold air filling my mouth and realise I am standing with my jaw open and muted.

The flowers escape my grasp, my hand empty of purpose, she pulls them towards her, and I hear a 'thank you.' I look up just in time to see the door closing, plundering me into shade which snaps me out of my trance.

'Rachel.' I say too loudly, causing her to swing the door open once again. 'Hi, again, I have come to see you,' I say slowly and pronounced, sounding creepy.

'Who are you?' she quizzically asks with a growing concern etched across her face.

'My name is Phil Jenkins, son of John Jenkins.'

I pause and wait for a reaction but nothing. 'He was close

friends with your mother once upon a time,' I say, biting my lip at the fairy tale reference.

Her eyes widen, and she brings her hand to her mouth, muffling, 'Oh my God.' Her shocked recollection ignites my smile, my relief.

'John, the fisherman from Devon?' She asks.

Fisherman? I replay her question in my head. She must be momentarily confused. 'He wasn't a fisherman, and he was from Dorset, not Devon.' Holding my smile, hiding my creeping insecurity, willing her acceptance.

Rachel's hand falls back to her side, and her shoulders drop, her bubble burst before fully inflated. It is clear from her reaction that the description she offered means something to her.

'Rachel, who is John? The fisherman from Devon? I ask because we may still be talking about the same man.'

It is Rachel's turn to stand motionless, reflecting and calculating before responding. 'I am sorry, nothing, err no-one, I don't know you and I do not know a John from Dorset, why are you here and what do you want?'

I see the irritation growing, none of this was how I envisaged our meeting, and I too feel myself getting flustered, my train of thought rocked. I can't think. I reach for my pocket, knowing the photograph is not there.

A shriek behind me breaks our silence; we both turn. 'Oh my god, it's you,' screams a girl standing on the pavement pointing to me.

'Mum, this man has just been in the shop, Ella served him, but I heard their conversation, he says he is your brother.'

Her pointing finger shining the brightest of spotlights on me. She looks familiar, but I pull my eyes away and turn back to meet Rachel's as the fill with emotion.

'She is right Rachel, we share the same dad, John Jenkins, and I am very sorry to be telling you like this, via your daughter and standing on the street.'

Rachel stares at me, looking straight through me, her smile long gone. The girl from the florist walks past me, to her mum and gently guides her inside the house to a room, she glances back to me, beckoning me with her hand. 'Come in,' she says softly.

We sit opposite each other, both perched on the edge of deep sofas. I allow myself a glance to the mantelpiece and notice framed pictures of a family of four. I return my eyes quickly to Rachel. I sit tight allowing her to make the first move, unsure of her temperament and respecting her space. She takes her eyes away from the flowers she still holds and focuses on me once again.

'How do you know? How can you be certain?'

I lock my hands together. *What did I rehearse?* 'I recently returned to my childhood home. Dad passed away last month, and his friends told me about you and Robbie.' I look for a signal at the reference to Robbie, but Rachel sits motionless.

'I was as shocked as you are right now. I had no idea. I found a couple of old photographs and tracked down your uncle Derek. He knew my dad, the two of them had an altercation once, and then there was all the court stuff, and I am assuming the years of cover-up.'

The girl hands Rachel a glass of water and turns to me, placing a drink in my hand before quickly leaving the room again. 'Do you have the photographs?' Rachel asks.

I curse to myself under my breath, with frustration all over again. 'No, not with me, I know I should have brought them, I left in such a rush. The most recent one was with you, Robbie, and dad on a walking trip, you looked about 12 or 13, and there were others when you were much younger on a beach, maybe Brixham, that's why you thought of Devon.' I raise my arms more in hope than confidence.

Rachel takes a cautious sip of her water, not taking her eyes off me. 'And how do you know my uncle Derek?'

'He found my dad through his freemason network and warned him off your mum, he and a guy called Pete or Peter. They were quite persuasive.'

A nod of understanding. 'That does sound like Derek and Pete, quite the pair of thugs in their day.'

I tense up again and grit my teeth preparing to tell the worst of my findings. 'Well, my dad was hardly a saint, he was not honest with your mum, and she discovered that all the time he was with her, and you, he was also married, living with us and playing happy families in Dorset.'

I watch the horror unfold on Rachel's face. She gulps her water and cradles the empty glass. 'I am so sorry Rachel.'

'This does not sound right.' She pauses and allows her heavy eyelids to close for a moment, recalling a scene from the past. 'Robbie and I always talked about tracking him down, but we never had much to go on, and mum went ballistic at the mention of the idea. She was never the most stable of people as it was.' A resigned shake of her head.

'My mum told us that our dad walked out when we were very young. He was a fisherman who later went missing at sea, presumed dead. Apart from an old picture we once found, we knew nothing about him.'

A crashing wave of doubt floods my whole body, scaring me.

'But Rachel, the picture of you and Robbie with dad walking

on the moors was taken when you were a teenager, yet you said he left when you were very young without further contact?'

Rachel edges forward with purpose on her chair, I see the realisation passing across her body, 'Yes, that's right,' a sternness in her voice at odds with her troubled eyes.

My heart begins to throb at the cage of my chest, fear racing through my veins which I mask by tightening my lips shut to hide my trembling.

Rachel leaps to her feet and stands suddenly very tall, cheeks flaring red, her eyes narrowing on me. 'Just who do you think you are?' she yells down on me.

'You expect me to believe that you would tell a stranger the most emotive of secrets, in my shop, and by sheer coincidence, my daughter can hear every word from the back room.'

She jabs her finger towards me. 'Then you march over to my house with a couple of basic facts that anybody with half a brain cell can find on the Internet, and your only reference is your good friend Derek. I have never trusted Derek or his low life friends.'

'What is in it for you?' She snarls and talks through her gritted teeth.

I sit muted, trying to process, wanting to deflect her anger, wanting to get out.

'You have some nerve coming here expecting me to believe a complete a stranger. And you messed up. New information for you, my father left when we were young, maybe he did go missing at sea, maybe he didn't, but I am certain of one thing, and that is I never saw him after he left us and certainly never went on weekend rambles with him and my brother as teenagers!'

Rachel slumps back down in her chair, like a balloon collapsing to the floor after the air released. Her head buries into her hands, and the muscles in her chin tremble. Her cries carry a rawness, the opening of a wound.

I try my best to make sense of everything she has just said. *My shop?* My eyes are instantly drawn to the flowers wrapped in plastic decorated with the name 'Love R Flowers'. My lungs burn, I am gasping for air. A million new thoughts going through my head, the florists, the blonde girl, the photograph, is this a set up? Who would do this? Donald?

I stand, but buckle under the weakness of my legs like spaghetti. I stagger slowly out of the room, through the hallway and out the front door, all thoughts numbed.

The fresh cooling air transports me to another place, the traffic on the road silenced but I sense its motion, the figure approaching me does so slowly, my vision blurred, my eyes fixed to the ground. I grab hold of the gate, and it holds me in return.

'Hi again, I am Annie, you know, you look so familiar.' My mind takes an age to register the voice and translate the words. I raise my head slowly, and our eyes meet.

'Hi Annie.' And now I remember that warming smile.

'We met at my dad's funeral in Baysworth.'

'Wow. Yes.' Her eyes widen, and eyebrows raise.

I see her all over again, standing in front of me at the funeral, her discrete fringe covering her eyebrows, her silent features, high cheek bones, soft handshake, *'I wish I had known this man.'*

'Love R Flowers did the flowers for the funeral, or to give our full name, Love Rachel's Flowers. And I am guessing that this is not all some weird coincidence?'

'Which one? Me calling in today to buy flowers? I did not notice the shop name or see your face in the back room. But you hand delivering flowers to my dad's funeral? I guess my dad no longer trusted fate or believed in keeping secrets beyond the grave.'

'Wow, this will make a good dinner party story one day,' Annie nods her head back to the house where her mum sits in silence. 'Family is an emotive subject to her. She always wants with us what she didn't have growing up, the family days out with mum, dad, and the kids, meals around the dinner table, board games on a wet Sunday afternoon. It drives my brother and me insane sometimes, but we know it means so much to her. She always closes up when we ask her about her childhood. I know Grandma was no saint and used to leave her and Robbie for days at a time to fend for themselves. Once, she even made mum lie to the police about being smacked around by an old boyfriend so that she could get some revenge on him. The guilt has lived with her ever since.'

Her words shake life into my body, my brain ignites once again, and my focus returns. I think of the consequences of lying to the police, and I see my dad sitting in his chair reading the restraining order.

'Here, check this out,' Annie invites me, holding her phone in front of me showing a picture of an older woman sitting at a bar with a pint of lager, and a cigarette in her mouth, wearing a cowboy hat and a grimace towards the camera. 'I bet your Grandma does not look like this.' I focus on the picture, not on her Grandma, but the quality of the image.

'Excuse me a moment Annie, I've got an idea.'

I pull out my mobile. 'Hello Roger, thank goodness you're in. I have a problem and need some help.'

I talk through my request and pace up and down the street telling Annie about Baysworth to pass the time. I am too apprehensive about returning to Rachel without first receiving a response. I stare down at my phone, pressing a button to illuminate the screen, willing the notification of a reply.

My phone pings with the incoming message *'sorry had to smash two windows to get in'* followed by two attachments loading on my phone.

Annie and I walk back into the house. She continues straight to the kitchen, and I walk back into the living room.

'I am so sorry Rachel. In all my excitement and rush to meet you, I did not think about how turning up like this, so ill-prepared would look from your perspective.' I crouch down next to her. 'I have something to show you,' holding my phone in front of her to display the picture from my dining room, the one taken on the moors.

She stares intensely at it before turning to me, her face devoid of colour once again, as if she has seen a ghost. 'This is your dad, this is John?' she asks, her face pure white.

'Yes, but why do you look so concerned?' I ask.

'Because I don't know this man as John, I know him as James, a friend of my uncle Derek's from the Navy. We met up with him a few times, and I always thought it was a little weird. Derek was with us on this day, he took this photograph.'

She knowingly taps the screen of the phone. 'I remember this man, James or John or whatever his real name was, took a big interest in us, asked Robbie and me lots of questions about school, about our friends, what we liked doing. He was nice to us, but we thought it was creepy. We thought for a while that he and Derek could have been gay, but all that time Derek knew and was arranging these secret meetings.'

Rachel twists her wedding ring back and forth, casting her mind back again, and her voice much softer now. 'We used to meet every month or so for about a year then one day he disappeared. It was after my mum and Derek had a huge falling out, and that was that, no more days out with Uncle Derek, no more bumping into his friend James in town, on the seafront, or the moors.'

We exchange a nervous smile, some familiarity giving us some common ground.

'I promise Rachel, I only met Derek for the first time yesterday, trying to find you. But can you see what this means? My dad tried. He tried to re-connect, in any way he could while tied by the restraining order which your mum inflicted on him. He was risking jail by just being there.'

'Oh my god.' Her eyes widen, pulling her hand over her mouth. 'The police interview. She, she...'

'It's okay, I know, your mum made you talk to them.' I rest my hand on hers.

A wave of relief passes through me, giving way to gratitude. Derek was risking the wrath of his sister and violating the court order to help my dad. My mind wanders back to his confused state and soulless room at Jubilee House, and I know exactly how to thank him. I picture the paintings of horse racing's three classic winners, Nijinski, Dancing Brave, and Shergar, all of which are gathering dust at home. They'd do far better on the walls of Jubilee House.

I focus once again on my phone held in front of us. I slide my thumb across the screen, revealing the next picture, my dad and the young blonde-haired girl at the beach. Rachel pulls it closer, its light beaming on her face. She springs to her feet and runs out the room, her exaggerated steps ascending the stairs crashing above me. I stand up, alone in the living room, confused. I take a few steps to look closer at the photographs on the mantelpiece.

'This is us,' Annie says from behind me, pointing to a family picture from a beach holiday. 'My dad, Andrew, is a surgeon at Bournemouth Royal Infirmary, obviously mum and I, and the cheeky face next to me is James, my little brother. All he does is play football, plays for Bournemouth youth team so he must be good, but probably not half as good as he says he is.'

I smile back at Annie, the description resonating with me. My eyes are drawn to an older picture at the end of the mantelpiece of a younger-looking Rachel and younger-looking man.

'This is my uncle Robbie, no recent pictures of him I am afraid. He went travelling to New Zealand after college and never came back.' I freeze, searching in her eyes for more.

'He met a girl there and opened up a bar in Wanaka on the South Island, still lives there with his now wife and two boys, we FaceTime a lot though, you will like Robbie, he is a fun guy.' I breathe out the air in relief.

We are disturbed by the sound of footsteps and turn to see Rachel at the door. Both hands in front of her, holding against her chest the same old photograph of dad and the little girl at the beach. I look back up at Rachel, her eyes drowning as pearl-shaped tears roll down her cheek, we take a step towards each other, and she throws her arms around me, holding me tight..

'Tell me about him, Phil,' she asks, and I take a step back to compose myself. My mind thinks back to dad and the funeral, stopping on the two eulogies I wrote, the two accounts of his life.

I take a deep breath and slowly begin. 'He was the life and soul, gregarious by nature, first to the bar to buy the drinks, would talk to anyone. He would make impromptu speeches when not his party as a show of support and affirmation rather than attention-seeking. A self-confessed man of the world. He was comfortable talking about most subjects. He was warm. He was genuine. He was admired....'

About the Author

Alan Agnew was born in Northern Ireland, to his protestant father and catholic mother during the height of the troubles and as a result, moved to England at a young age. He was brought up in Godalming, Surrey and degree educated in Sweden. He has lived in Dubai, Sydney, New York and Amsterdam, and is currently residing in Singapore.

Home for Truths is his debut novel.

You can connect with me on:
- https://www.alanagnew.com
- https://twitter.com/AlanAgnewAuthor
- https://www.facebook.com/AlanAgnewAuthor